ISOBEL STEWART

NOR ALL
YOUR TEARS

Complete and Unabridged

LINFORD
Leicester

First published in Great Britain in 1974 by
Robert Hale & Company
London

First Linford Edition
published 2008
by arrangement with
Robert Hale Limited
London

British Library CIP Data

Stewart, Isobel
　　Nor all your tears.—Large print ed.—
Linford romance library
　　1. Amnesiacs—Fiction 2. Traffic accident
victims—Fiction 3. Recovered memory—
Fiction 4. Love stories 5. Large type books
　　I. Title
　　823.9′14 [F]

　　ISBN 978–1–84782–455–4

Published by
F. A. Thorpe (Publishing)
Anstey, Leicestershire

Set by Words & Graphics Ltd.
Anstey, Leicestershire
Printed and bound in Great Britain by
T. J. International Ltd., Padstow, Cornwall

'For my husband'

1

Afterwards, Christine wondered how long she had been there, sitting on the park bench in the rain.

Her head was aching, and she looked around her, bewildered and confused.

'What am I thinking of?' she wondered, closing her eyes as the tight band around her forehead ached even more. 'Sitting here in the rain, and letting Jenny get so wet.'

She stood up, and looked for the child.

'Jenny — Jenny!' she called, urgently, expecting to see the gay scarlet raincoat, with Jenny's fair pigtails bouncing under the scarlet cap, through the wet trees, coming towards her.

'Jenny?' Christine called again. 'It's time to go home.'

It was only then that she realized just how quiet and deserted it was, here in the park in the rain. She went through the wet trees to the swings, where Jenny usually played, but there was no one there. She could feel her mouth drying, her heart thudding unevenly with panic.

She stood still for a moment, looking around her at the park and the children's playground, silent and deserted in the rain. It's all right, she told herself, it must be all right. She was here just a moment ago, she — she can't be far away.

'Jenny!' she called again, and now she could hear the distress in her voice.

Then, at the far end of the playground, she saw a movement in the little hut that sold ice cream in summer. Thankfully, she ran across the wet grass.

'Jenny,' she called, 'come along, darling, we must get home.'

But it wasn't Jenny.

Two small boys looked at her, their eyes wide. Christine tried to control her distress.

'Have you seen a little girl?' she asked

them, forcing herself to keep her voice steady.

They both looked back at her, not saying anything.

'A little girl of — of seven,' Christine said. 'With long fair hair, and a red raincoat.'

The bigger of the boys shook his head.

'No girls here,' he told her. 'Only Sammy and me.'

Christine stared at him, panic rising again.

'But she was here,' she said, shakily. 'She — she was playing while I sat down. It wasn't raining then. She must be here.'

'What's her name?' the boy asked, interestedly, and Christine's heart leapt.

'Jenny,' she told him.

He shook his head again.

'Me and Sam don't know any girls called Jenny,' he said. He jerked his head at the smaller boy. 'Come on, Sam, time to go home.'

They went off, without a backward glance.

Christine turned back to the swings, hoping against hope that somehow she had just missed seeing Jenny, that now she would be there, her small impish face smiling at the game she had played with her mother.

But there was no Jenny.

The park-keeper, Christine thought. If she's wandered away and got lost, then someone would take her to him. That's what must have happened.

She hurried along the path, wet and slippery with fallen leaves now rain-soaked. And all the time she looked from side to side, hoping that through the trees there would be a glimpse of a small girl in a scarlet raincoat, looking for her mother.

The park-keeper was new, not the old man who had been in charge since she used to bring Jenny here in her pram.

'Please — ' Christine said, breathlessly, and he looked up, surprised, then put down his steaming mug of tea.

'Something wrong, lady?' he asked.

'It's my little girl,' Christine told him,

4

trying to speak calmly, reasonably. 'She — she was with me, beside the playground, and — and now she's gone.'

'She'll be playing around some-where,' the man said, reasonably. 'Can't be far away.'

Christine shook her head.

'I've called and I've called,' she said, and now it was impossible to speak steadily. 'There's no sign of her, and two little boys who were there said that they hadn't seen her.'

He looked at her, and there was something in his glance that made her suddenly uncomfortable.

'What were you doing?' he asked. 'Could you see her all the time?'

Christine hesitated.

'I was sitting on the bench,' she told him, slowly. 'Where I always sit. I — I had this awful headache, and I didn't notice that it was raining. Then — then when I looked for Jenny, she wasn't there.'

He looked at her again.

'It's been raining a long time,' he pointed out. 'Look how wet you are. If you sat there in the rain, and took no notice of the kid, she must have gone to get shelter somewhere.'

Christine shook her head.

'It wasn't like that,' she said, her voice low. 'I often sit there while Jenny plays. Today I — I had a dreadful headache, I may have closed my eyes. But I can't understand why she didn't come to me when the rain began.'

'Do you want me to call the police, lady?' the park-keeper asked, his hand on the telephone.

Christine looked at him, all her unworded fears suddenly, shatteringly brought into the open.

'No — no,' she said, shakily. 'There can't be anything wrong. I'll go back and have another look. She must be there.' At the door of the hut, she turned back to him. 'If she comes here — if anyone brings her, please keep her here. I'll come back if I don't find her.'

It was raining even harder as she

hurried back the way she had come. Jenny must be there, she told herself. There was no reason why she shouldn't be. She — she must have just wandered away, hadn't heard her mother's voice because of the rain.

Breathlessly, Christine turned the corner, certain that Jenny would be there, her fair pigtails wet under her red cap, her small snub nose wet with raindrops, perhaps her lip trembling a little now.

'Jenny — Jenny!' she called, loudly, not caring whether anyone else heard her, caring for nothing but the thought of Jenny, lost and frightened somewhere. Beyond that, her thoughts didn't dare go.

But Jenny wasn't there.

The wind blew Christine's scarf off her head, and she stood in the driving rain, her thoughts whirling. Where could Jenny have gone? Where would she think of going?

And now there was no more hiding from the dark fears rising inside her.

What if Jenny hadn't gone anywhere — of her own free will? She was only a little girl, only seven, and although she wasn't supposed to talk to strangers, she was a friendly child, a little girl whose confident trust had never been betrayed. No one could tempt her with sweets, but — a dog, a cat, one of the squirrels in the park — anyone interested in any animal would win her friendship.

Christine pressed her hands to her aching forehead. I'll have to go to the police, she thought, all at once exhausted, fear draining away all her strength.

And then it came to her.

Of course. The park was quite near Adam's office. Jenny must have decided to go and see her father. And — and right now, Adam was probably trying to phone home, to tell her that Jenny was with him, to tell her not to worry.

Relief swept over her, making her dizzy, and she wondered why she hadn't thought of that right away. But the sudden shock of seeing that Jenny wasn't there had prevented her from thinking clearly. Even now the shock of it was still going on and on in her aching head — She isn't there. Jenny isn't there. Where is she?

Her hair was wet now, and the scarf too wet to put on again, but Christine didn't care, as she hurried out of the top gate of the park. The rush-hour traffic hurtled on its way along the busy street, and there was another stab of fear as she thought of a small girl crossing here. She knows only to cross at the zebra crossing, she told herself. She — she wouldn't try anywhere else.

She made for the zebra crossing herself, and then, just before she reached it, there, on the far side of the street, she saw a child in a scarlet raincoat. Jenny — it must be Jenny.

Without any thought in her mind but her child, Christine turned. There was one moment when she saw the car bearing down on her, saw the driver's white, horrified face.

★ ★ ★

She knew the car had hit her, knew she had been badly hurt, knew she was in hospital.

Often, swimming out of a sea of pain, she would see a nurse bending over her, and she would try to speak, try to tell them about Jenny, tell them to get Adam.

But no words would come, and soon the nurse, talking to her soothingly, trying to calm her down, would give her an injection, and the pain would recede, and there would be only the terror and the anxiety for Jenny.

Sometimes, there were other people. A man she knew must be a doctor, another man she thought was a policeman. They were questioning her, but she didn't really know what they were asking her. Their voices were so far away, and their faces swam mistily in front of her. She tried to ask them, too, about Jenny, and when she couldn't, when no words would come,

10

her forehead would grow cold and damp with distress, so that the doctor would take the other man away, and there would be another injection, another period of blankness.

Once, surprising herself, she said Jenny's name.

'Jenny.'

It was only a whisper, but she heard herself say it, and when the young nurse came hurrying over she tried again. But this time nothing came, no matter how hard she tried.

'Please try,' the girl said, her young face anxious. 'Just tell us your name, and where you live.'

It was only then that Christine began to realise. They didn't even know who she was. Slowly, painfully, she sorted out the rest. That meant that Adam didn't know what had happened, didn't know where she was. And Jenny. Had it been Jenny she saw across the street, going to her father's office? If it was — Jenny, at home, crying herself to sleep because her mother wasn't there.

And — if it wasn't Jenny, then where was she?

Christine tried to say her name, but she couldn't. She closed her eyes and turned her head to the side, slow tears running down her cheeks. Gently, the young nurse wiped her face.

'Don't distress yourself,' she said softly. 'Have a sleep — soon you'll be able to tell us.'

Christine wasn't sure, afterwards, just how long it was before she was able to speak to them, but it seemed that there were days and nights of half-consciousness, days and nights when the dreadful helplessness of being unable to communicate with anyone, of being unable to ask for Adam, to find out about Jenny, engulfed her, so that it was easier to let go, easier to slip away again into oblivion.

And then one day she woke to feel the sun on her face. She remembered the rain, the day Jenny was lost, and she knew that unless she made a superhuman effort, no one else could do anything more for her.

She must have made a small sound, for the young nurse was beside her right away.

'Jenny,' Christine said, and although it was a whisper, she knew it was clear.

The girl's eyes widened.

'Jenny,' she repeated and Christine nodded.

'She was lost,' she said, with an effort. 'In the park. She — wasn't there.'

The girl leaned nearer to her.

'Just tell me your name,' she suggested, easily. 'Then we'll find out about Jenny.'

For a moment, Christine closed her eyes, gathering everything in her to tell them, to end this nightmare of uncertainty and anxiety.

'Christine,' she murmured. 'Christine Lawrence.'

'And your address?' the girl asked.

'18 Arthur's Crescent,' she whispered. 'Please — get Adam.'

She didn't know whether they had given her another injection then, or whether the effort was too much for her, but although she tried to fight it, the waves of unconsciousness eventually overcame her.

When she awoke, Adam was there, sitting in the chair beside the bed.

She said his name, hazily, and he turned to her.

'Adam — is Jenny all right?' she asked, her tongue still thick with sleep, her mind fogged, clinging only to this. 'We were in the park, and it was raining, and — Adam, when I looked for her, she wasn't there.'

Suddenly, incredibly, after the days and nights of being unable to say anything, it was all right.

'I asked everyone,' she told him shakily. 'I asked if they'd seen a little girl in a scarlet raincoat, but they hadn't.'

For a moment, there was something strange in his grey eyes as he looked down at her, something that alarmed her, that made her breath catch in her throat.

'It's all right, Christine,' he said carefully, after a moment, after a swift glance at the doctor, who was beside the window. 'Jenny is all right.'

'Where is she?' Christine asked, urgently, distressed by the strangeness of his look.

Again, there was that moment of hesitation, of exchanged glances, before Adam spoke.

'Jenny is fine, Christine,' he told her. 'She's at home.'

Her eyes searched his face, and she knew that he was telling her the truth. And yet — there was something that bothered her.

'I want to see her,' she murmured, exhaustion suddenly overcoming her.

'Not now, Mrs Lawrence,' the doctor said decisively, coming forward. 'You have to concentrate on getting better. Your daughter is all right, I promise you that. I think you should go, Mr Lawrence — she's very tired. Still a long way to go.'

'I'm not tired,' Christine protested

15

foggily. 'Adam — don't go.'

'I'll be back soon,' he promised, standing beside her. For a moment, he hesitated and then he bent down and his lips brushed her cheek, lightly.

After he had gone, she couldn't fight the tiredness any longer. But as she fell asleep, the last thought that was with her was that Jenny was all right. Adam had said so, and the doctor had said so. Jenny was all right.

She clung to that thought in the following days, as her strength gradually returned to her and she began to find out the extent of her injuries. Her left arm had been broken, three ribs broken, and she had been badly concussed. The young nurse told her she was lucky to be alive, and Christine, remembering the days and nights of pain, the utter impossibility of finding the strength even to say her name, knew that this was true. But what she couldn't understand was why Adam hadn't found her, although she couldn't give his name.

She asked him, one afternoon when he was visiting her, and again there was the strange clouding-over of his eyes.

'It isn't as easy as that, Christine,' he said after a moment.

'I don't see why not,' she returned. 'There aren't so many hospitals in Edinburgh. If you asked at them all — '

'It wasn't as easy as that,' Adam told her, firmly. 'Now stop worrying, Christine. It's all sorted out now, and that's all you need to know.'

'Why can't I see Jenny?' she asked again, as she had so often asked.

'Because the doctor and I both feel it would be upsetting for you and for Jenny.' He smiled, and his voice was warm and teasing. 'Look at you, honey — all plastered and bandaged, with your hair only just growing properly again — it wouldn't be very nice for Jenny to see you like that.'

'I don't see why not,' Christine returned, stubbornly. 'She isn't a baby — she's seven, and she's a sensible child. If she knows I've been in an accident, she knows I'll be bandaged. I don't see what harm it could do for her to see me.'

'No, Christine,' Adam said, decisively. 'This is doctor's orders, and there's no arguing about it.'

But Christine wasn't giving up that easily.

'I suppose she's with Valerie?' she asked.

Again, there was the momentary flicker in Adam's grey eyes, the almost imperceptible pause.

'Yes,' he said, carefully, 'she's with Valerie.'

'It's nice of Valerie to look after her,' Christine told him, meaning it. 'But I'm sure as a nurse she realizes too that it would be better to let Jenny see me.'

'No, Christine,' Adam said again, quite gently. 'Valerie realizes too that it's better to wait for a bit.

She closed her eyes, suddenly tired.

'Valerie would agree with anything you say,' she murmured, knowing she sounded sulky. 'She always does.'

'What do you mean?' Adam asked.

'Just because she's your cousin, she thinks you're the absolute authority.'

Unexpectedly, Adam laughed.

'Which you obviously don't,' he teased her, lightly. He bent down and kissed her. Christine, overcome by compunction, put up her hand and touched his fair hair.

'Adam,' she said, surprised. 'You're going grey, just at the temples here.'

She touched the grey part gently.

'Why haven't I noticed it before?' she asked him. And then a thought struck her. 'Was this because you were worried about me?' she said, her breath catching in her throat at the thought of Adam being so worried that his hair turned grey.

He hesitated.

'You could say that,' he agreed.

He straightened.

'Would you like Valerie to come and see you?' he asked. 'The doctor says she can.'

'No — not Valerie.'

It was a swift, instinctive reaction, surprising Christine herself. And yet, looking at Adam, she had the strange conviction that it hadn't surprised him. Embarrassed at the way she had said this she felt she had to justify it.

'If I'm not allowed to have Jenny, I don't want anyone else,' she said quickly.

Adam shrugged.

'As you like,' he returned, indifferently. 'But you don't need to worry about Jenny — Valerie can take care of her with no trouble.'

It was only when Christine had been allowed out of bed, to move around the so-familiar little room, that she realized that Adam hadn't told her anything of what had happened to Jenny that day.

As soon as he came that evening, she asked him.

'You didn't ever tell me what really happened the day Jenny was lost,' she said to him.

He took one of the black grapes he had brought her.

'You didn't ask me,' he countered.

Christine thought about this, realizing that as soon as she knew that Jenny was safe at home she hadn't worried about how she had got there.

'Did she come to the office?' she asked.

Again, there was the brief hesitation, before Adam nodded.

'But why did she go away from the park?' Christine asked, frowning. 'She shouldn't have done that, Adam, it was very naughty. You — you've no idea how worried I was.'

Her voice shook, remembering the dreadful helplessness in the park, the bewildering panic, the words in her mind — She isn't there. Jenny isn't there. Where is she?

Adam sat down beside her and took her free hand in both of his. And when his hands closed around hers, there was a sudden, strange bewilderment, a bewilderment that slipped away from her and eluded her before she could even grasp it. Something to do with the shape of his hands, with the touch of them. And then it was gone, when he spoke.

'Suppose you tell me everything you can about that afternoon in the park, Christine,' he said, and the casualness of his voice didn't deceive her.

'I know what you're thinking,' she whispered, and sudden unexpected tears filled her eyes. 'You're thinking that — that I didn't look after Jenny properly, that I sat there and didn't notice that she had gone.'

'No, honey, you mustn't think that,' he replied. 'I just want to know what you remember of the whole afternoon.'

Christine closed her eyes.

'I remember everything,' she said, wearily. 'I had this awful headache, and I sat down on the park bench. I — didn't notice that it was raining, and then when I did I called for Jenny. I called and called, but — she wasn't there.' In spite of herself, her voice shook, as she remembered.

'And before that?' Adam asked, casually. 'What did you and Jenny do before you went to the park?'

She stared at him.

'We — we were shopping,' she said quickly, after a moment. 'Yes, we were shopping, and — and we went home by the park, and then I had this headache and — '

Adam was looking at her, his grey eyes holding hers, and Christine's voice trailed off.

'You don't remember, do you, honey?' he asked her.

Christine bit her lip.

'No,' she admitted, slowly, with an effort. 'No, Adam, I don't remember.'

His hand tightened on hers.

'What is the first thing you remember about that afternoon in the park, Christine?' he asked her. 'Think hard.'

Christine thought, forcing her mind back to the park, the rain on the trees, the bench she had been sitting on. And finding that Jenny wasn't there. 'I remember — ' she began, slowly, trying to pinpoint that first moment of realization.

Adam leaned forward, his grey eyes intent on her.

Christine closed her eyes.

'I — Adam, I don't remember anything before suddenly realizing that it was raining, and — and that Jenny wasn't there,' she said at last shakily.

'You mean you don't remember coming into the park?' Adam asked.

She shook her head.

'Or leaving home earlier — with Jenny with you?' he asked, insistently.

'There were so many times when Jenny and I went out, I — I'm not sure which time I'm thinking of,' she replied, after a while.

Adam leaned back.

'So in fact,' he said, 'you don't remember anything except having this headache, and finding yourself in the park, with Jenny gone?'

Christine looked up at him, and now she wasn't even trying to hide her fear from him.

'But it's a dreadful thing to happen, Adam, just — just forgetting everything like that. Something could really have happened to Jenny, if she hadn't had the sense to come to you.'

His hand covered hers for a moment, and again, there was that brief and bewildering sense of strangeness, gone almost as soon as it had come.

'Don't worry, honey, it isn't something you can do anything about. It must have been that bad headache you had.'

Christine tried to smile, but tears were very near.

'Lend me your hanky, Adam — I need a good blow.'

He took the white handkerchief out of his pocket, and as he did so, a small white card fell on to the bed. Quickly, he lifted it up, but not before Christine had seen what was written on it. She looked up at him, bewildered.

'Adam, why does it give our address as Jenner Street?'

He laughed.

'Christine honey, that was meant to

be a surprise We've moved. While you were — ill.'

The momentary pause made her wonder, but there was too much else to wonder about. All at once, distress and anxiety were too much for her. She felt her heart thudding against her ribs, and she felt her forehead becoming clammy. From a great distance, she could hear Adam's voice.

'Christine? Honey, it's all right, don't upset yourself, you'll like the house, it's much nicer. I — was going to tell you later, just before you came home. Here — have a drink of water.'

She drank the water, and gradually the panic subsided. She leaned back on her pillows, able to speak normally again.

'But Adam, Jenner Street is so far from school for Jenny. I — I wish you had consulted me first. You know we always liked her being near enough to walk round by herself. How is she going to manage from the other side of town?'

Adam stood up.

'Christine, there's no need to worry, I promise you that,' he told her, firmly. 'I did this for the best, you must believe that.' He smiled, but she saw that the smile didn't reach his eyes, still watching her intently. 'Now I'm going — I seem to have upset you enough for today.' He kissed her cheek, lightly. 'You see how right I am not to let you see Jenny, when you're still so easily upset? You must realize it wouldn't do her any good to see you like this.'

Defeated, Christine turned away from him.

'I wouldn't be like this if I could see Jenny,' she said, her voice low. But he pretended not to hear her, as he rang the bell for the nurse.

'Hello, Nurse Johnson,' he said, smiling at the pretty red-haired young nurse. 'I'm in the dog-box because I've moved house without telling my wife — all to surprise her and give her a nice easily-run house when she comes home. I think you'd better give her something to calm her down. Dr

Ruthven said she wasn't to get excited.'

Swiftly, professionally, the young nurse lifted Christine's right wrist, and took her pulse. Christine began to speak, to say that she didn't need anything to calm her down, but Nurse Johnson put the thermometer in her mouth. While she stood there, her eyes on her big watch, Christine looked at Adam, standing beside the door, easy and relaxed, and suddenly she was angry with him.

'I think you should go now, Mr Lawrence,' the young nurse told him, taking the thermometer from Christine's mouth. 'Your wife really should have a rest now.'

When he had gone, she settled Christine against the pillows, easing her arm and the strapping around her ribs, so that she was comfortable. Christine lay still, unprotesting, for a thought had come to her.

'I'd like you to have a good rest, Mrs Lawrence,' Nurse Johnson said briskly. She smiled. 'Then maybe you'll feel like thanking your husband for such a nice surprise. You know, we'll all be sorry when you go — not just because we'll miss you, but because we like Mr Lawrence coming. He's absolutely dishy — must be marvellous to be married to a fab man like that.'

Still angry with Adam, it was all Christine could do to manage a smile.

'That thick fair hair, and his eyes, in that tan!' She looked down at Christine. 'You must have lost your tan more quickly than he has.'

'Lost my tan?' Christine repeated, puzzled.

'From your skiing holiday,' the girl said, tucking in the sheets firmly.

The pulse in Christine's throat began to beat unevenly again.

'We haven't been on any skiing holiday,' she told the young nurse.

For a moment, the girl's blue eyes looked into hers, appraisingly, then the girl turned away.

'No?' she murmured. 'I — must have misunderstood your husband.' She straightened up. 'Have a good rest, Mrs Lawrence. If you're a good girl, Dr Ruthven may let you get up for a little while tomorrow.

She had reached the door when Christine called her back.

'Nurse,' she said quickly, casually, 'I was wondering — couldn't you get them to plug a phone in, so that I could phone my little girl?'

'I'm sorry, Mrs Lawrence,' the girl replied after a moment, 'Dr Ruthven gave orders specifically that you weren't to make any phone calls.'

Christine closed her eyes as the young nurse went out. So much for that idea. She'd have to wait until she was up and allowed to move around, and then phone Jenny from one of the public phones in the hospital.

The day after that, the plaster was taken off her arm, and she was allowed out of bed for a little. But even sitting in the armchair by the window exhausted her, and she was almost frightened by her image in the mirror. I look so much older, she thought, dismayed. And then she remembered the grey hairs at Adam's temple, and she was ashamed. Her accident had aged him too — and he had had all the worry of the first few days, of not knowing where she was. Poor Adam — trying so hard to please her with the new house, and she had been so ungrateful. But she thought, wistfully, of the house in Arthur's Crescent, with all its memories. Jenny's pram, under the old apple tree. The wonderful view of Castle Rock from the bay window of the lounge. Jenny's first steps, on the lawn outside the kitchen. So many memories.

I'll go back, she promised herself. After I'm home, and better, Jenny and I will go back one day and look at it. Her school is near there, I'll meet her and we'll walk up Arthur's Crescent and look at the house.

Each day she was allowed up for a little longer, allowed to walk across the room. Her arm was regaining strength all the time, once she began doing the excercises the physiotherapist recommended. Nurse Johnson suggested that the hairdresser who came twice a week to the hospital, should come and do her hair, and Christine enjoyed this. On an impulse, she asked the girl to cut her hair short, and when she looked at herself in the mirror, with her brown hair short and casual, her blue eyes less anxious, less strained, she was pleased.

So was Adam.

'That's my Christine again,' he said when he came in with Dr Ruthven that evening. He bent over her, and this time, instead of kissing her cheek, his lips brushed hers, lightly. And suddenly, instinctively, everything in Christine recoiled, so that she drew back from her husband, her lips cold against his. The next moment, warm colour flooded her cheeks as she realized what she had done.

'I'm — sorry, Adam,' she whispered, with difficulty.

He shrugged, but his grey eyes were

thoughtful, appraising. And Christine saw the doctor, too, look at her questioningly, for he couldn't have avoided seeing what she had done.

Adam didn't stay long that evening, and Christine was ashamed of the relief she felt when he left her. Tomorrow, she told herself, I am going to phone Jenny. I've had enough of this. Tomorrow, even if they won't let me see her, at least I will talk to her, tell her I'm all right, tell her I'll be home soon.'

She had to wait for the right time, for she wasn't supposed to be out of her room without a nurse. But in the early afternoon, in the rest hour before visiting time, the hospital was quiet, with few nurses around. She stood at the door of her room, waiting, watching. The phone, fortunately, wasn't far away, just round the corner. She had money to make the call, for she had asked Adam a few days ago to leave her some, in case she wanted sweets from the trolley.

Her legs were trembling when she

reached the phone booth, but no one had seen her. She dialled the number. And it was only when a strange voice answered that she realized. Sick disappointment swept over her. How could she have been so stupid?

'I'm sorry,' she said, breathlessly. 'I — I wanted to speak to Mr Lawrence. I forgot that he had moved. Could you give me his new telephone number, please?'

'Mr Lawrence?' the voice at the other end repeated, doubtfully. 'I'm sorry I can't help you. You must have got the wrong number.'

'Don't you have his new telephone number?' Christine asked desperately.

There was a moment's silence, and then the voice said firmly that she must have the wrong number, and she should try the phone book. Frustrated, Christine replaced the receiver. How could it be in the phone book, when they had just moved? And surely Adam had left their new number with the people who had bought the old house?

She rang Enquiries, and asked for the number of Lawence, Adam, giving the new address in Jenner Street. The girl gave her the number and she dialled it, weak with relief.

Let it be Jenny who answers, she prayed, just let me hear her voice, hear her say Mummy to me.

But it was Valerie's voice that answered, giving the number in her cool and assured voice.

'Can I speak to Jenny?' Christine said quietly, evenly, not giving her name.

There was a moment's pause. Then Valerie spoke, and she knew that she had lost.

'It is Christine, isn't it?' she asked, and now her voice was warm. 'Christine dear, I'm sure you shouldn't be out of bed phoning.'

'I — just wanted to talk to Jenny,' Christine said, knowing her disappointment was in her voice, and not caring.

There was another pause.

'I am sorry, Christine,' Valerie said, regretfully. 'But Jenny isn't in. And

— Adam did say it would be better for you to wait until you come home, didn't he?'

She was still speaking when Christine put the phone down, saying she hoped that Christine would soon be home, saying what a dreadful time it had been. But Christine, sick with disappointment, didn't care. Slowly, she made her way back along the corridor and into bed. And lying there, unable to sleep, the conviction and the certainty grew in her that there was something wrong, something they weren't telling her. Something wrong with Jenny.

That night, when Adam came, she asked him again. She knew that Valerie would have told him about the phone call, so there was no point in trying to hide it.

'You know I phoned?' she asked him, more abruptly than she had intended to, when he came in.

'Yes, Valerie told me,' he replied. He took both her hands in his. 'Christine, you must believe that we know what is

36

best for you. You've been very ill — you can't rush things.'

Christine withdrew her hands from his.

'There's something wrong with Jenny, isn't there?' she asked him, her eyes searching his face, searching for whatever it was that he was trying to hide from her. 'I know there is — there must be.'

'There's nothing wrong with Jenny,' he told her, steadily.

'Then why won't you let me see her?' she asked desperately, not knowing that she was crying until she felt the salt taste of tears on her lips. 'You say she's all right, but Adam, you don't know how I worry, lying here, remembering that day in the park when I couldn't find her. Adam, you must let me see her, I'm going out of my mind worrying about what is wrong.'

She didn't know that he had rung for the nurse until she was there, her face concerned as she bent over Christine. But Christine was past caring now, and the tears ran down her face, unheeded. Then Dr Ruthven was there, a syringe in his hand.

'What is it, Mrs Lawrence?' he asked, concerned.

She turned to him.

'They won't let me see Jenny,' she told him through her tears. 'They won't let me see her, and I know something's wrong, I know something must have happened to her that day in the park when I couldn't find her.'

She saw the quick glance that the doctor exchanged with Adam, and somehow this confirmed her fears.

'Mrs Lawrence,' the doctor said, and when she turned away he repeated her name, more loudly. 'Mrs Lawrence, I promise you that your daughter is safe and well. There is nothing wrong with her. I'm giving you something now to calm you down and to make you sleep, and tomorrow we'll talk about this again.'

There was the stab of the hypodermic, and then the familiar woolly feeling. Christine tried to fight against the waves of drowsiness, but it was no use. But as she gave in, she heard the doctor's voice, faint and far-off now.

'We cannot put it off any longer, Mr Lawrence, she must be told. I suggest you come tomorrow and I'll be here too.'

She heard Adam say something, but she couldn't hear what it was. And then there was nothing more.

They came the next morning after breakfast, Adam and Dr Ruthven together. Christine, still a little dazed and drugged, was nevertheless determined to be up and sitting in the armchair when they came.

She looked from one to the other, Adam, sitting on the edge of the bed, his grey eyes on her, concerned and yet — watchful, she thought, at the same time. And Dr Ruthven, his grey hair untidy as always, his surprisingly bright blue eyes on her face.

'Mrs Lawrence,' he said, firmly, 'the first thing you must believe is that your daughter is all right. I promise you that. Do you believe me?'

Christine looked at the blue eyes, wise and kind.

'I believe you,' she replied, her voice low.

'Good. Then you hold on to that. Just remember that she is all right. Will you do that?'

Bewildered, anxious, Christine agreed.

'This isn't easy,' the doctor said after a moment, running his hand through his hair. 'Mr Lawrence, I think it's up to you now — just tell her simply.'

Adam came across and sat on the arm of the chair, one hand lightly on her shoulders.

'I don't know how to begin, Christine,' he said, worriedly. 'We can't put this off any longer, I see that.'

She looked at him silently, unable to speak, holding desperately on to what the doctor had said — that Jenny was all right.

'That day in the park, Christine,' Adam began, slowly, 'when you couldn't find

Jenny — ' He stopped, and tried again. 'Christine, you were looking for a little girl of seven, a little girl in a scarlet raincoat.'

'I — I was looking for Jenny,' Christine said, through stiff lips.

For a moment, Adam's eyes met the doctor's, and then he turned to her.

'Jenny is seventeen, Christine,' he said slowly, deliberately. 'Not seven. Seventeen.'

She couldn't understand him. He was saying that Jenny was seventeen. But Jenny was seven, he must know that.

'Jenny is seventeen,' Adam said again. 'Ten years ago, Christine, you walked out of the house, leaving me and leaving Jenny. I — until the hospital contacted me, and I came here, that was the last I saw of you.'

Bewildered, Christine turned to the doctor.

'What is he saying?' she asked, shakily. 'I — I don't understand what he means.'

'I'm sorry, Mrs Lawrence,' the doctor said, and the pity and the sympathy in his voice brought tears to her eyes. 'It isn't easy for you to understand, I know that. I wish there was some way of making it easier for you.'

Christine took a deep breath, trying to steady herself, trying to control the wild leaping of her heart.

'Are you trying to tell me that it's ten years since I've seen you or Jenny, Adam?' she asked, her eyes on his face. 'That I — walked out and left you ten years ago?'

He nodded.

'But — I wouldn't do that,' Christine murmured, almost to herself. 'I would never leave Jenny.'

And it was only afterwards that she remembered saying that, remembered the significance of it.

'I'm afraid you did,' Adam said, evenly.

'But why?' Christine asked him, bewildered. 'Why should I leave you?'

He turned away.

'If I had known that, Christine, it would have saved me years of anguish,' he said, quietly.

'Oh, Adam,' she murmured, unsteadily. 'Adam, I don't know what to say. I — I can't quite grasp it, even now. How can a thing like this happen?'

'We don't know, Mrs Lawrence,' Dr Ruthven said, his voice warm, sympathetic. 'I wish we could give you some reasonable explanation of it. But you see now why we couldn't let you see your daughter. After the severity of your accident, you just couldn't take a shock like that.'

Jenny — seventeen. Not a little girl of seven, with freckles on her snub little nose, with long fair pigtails, but a girl of seventeen, almost grown up.

It was then that full realization came to Christine. She would never again see the little girl she had searched for so desperately in the park that rainy day. That little girl was gone, ten years ago. Gone for ever.

She was crying then, silent, desperate

tears. Crying for Adam, left alone and bewildered all these years ago. Crying for Jenny, left without her mother, growing up without her mother. And crying for herself, for the lost years.

She didn't know how long it was before her tears stopped, and she looked up at the two men.

'But where have I been?' she asked them, bewildered. 'Where have I been for these ten years?'

For a moment, the two men looked at each other, and then Adam spoke, gently. 'We don't know, Christine,' he told her. 'We don't know where you've been.'

2

It was a long time before Christine could say anything.

She looked from her husband to the doctor, and still she could hardly grasp the full horror of what they had just told her.

'Ten years!' she said at last, unsteadily. 'And — I don't remember a thing. I don't know where I've been, what I've done.' She looked directly at Adam. 'I — I don't know why I left you, ten years ago, but — I'm sorry, Adam.'

He said nothing, and she thought, with shame, that it was too late now to say sorry. Long ago — many years ago — he had had to learn to live with the knowledge that his wife had walked out on him and on their child.

'Who looked after Jenny?' she asked him. 'I mean — when it happened, when she was small.'

'Valerie did,' he told her.

Of course, she might have realized that, Christine told herself. Valerie, Adam's cousin, was the obvious person to take care of Jenny. She forced down the sudden stab resentment, reminding herself that she had left Jenny, and someone had to look after a little girl of seven left without her mother.

She turned to the doctor.

'Will I remember where I was?' she asked him, trying to keep her voice steady. 'I — surely I can't go through the rest of my life with a gap of ten years?'

'I can't say, Mrs Lawrence,' the doctor told her, and his blue eyes held hers levelly, honestly. 'Something may just click, and you might have the complete picture. But — there's no guarantee that that will happen, no certainty that you will ever remember.' He patted her hand. 'I'm going to leave you with your husband for a little while, my dear, I'm sure there are many things you want to talk about.' He looked at

Adam. 'Don't stay too long, Mr Lawrence — I know after this your wife will want to get home as soon as possible, and she still needs a few days here with plenty rest.'

When the door closed behind him, Christine found herself wishing he had stayed, wishing, suddenly, that she and Adam weren't alone together. She turned to the window, looking out, but unseeing, seeing again herself running through the rain-wet paths in the park, looking for Jenny. Looking for Jenny, whom she hadn't seen for ten years.

'Well, Christine?' Adam said at last, gently.

Her eyes filled with tears.

'Adam, I don't know what to say.' With an effort, she steadied her voice. 'I don't know why I left you and Jenny ten years ago, and — I don't know why I came back.'

'Don't worry, honey,' Adam said, after a moment. 'You mustn't force yourself to try to remember anything — just wait until it comes.'

But she couldn't leave it alone.

'The day of the accident,' she said, slowly, working it out. 'Surely I had a handbag or something with me — something to say who I was?'

Adam shook his head.

'I believe that's the first thing the police thought of,' he told her, regretfully. 'But there was nothing. They think it's possible that it was thrown from you when the car hit you, and — someone may have taken it.'

He leaned forward and took both her hands in his.

'Don't worry about it, Christine,' he said again. 'You'll only make yourself ill with worrying. Just accept that it happened, and — that you're back.'

But it wasn't as easy as that. In the next few days, as she gradually re-gained her strength, Christine found that it was impossible not to keep on wondering. How could ten years of a person's life be lost just like that? Surely there was someone, somewhere, who was looking for her, who was wondering where she had disappeared to, why she hadn't come home that day?

And more than that, she thought about what had happened ten years ago. Ten years ago, when she had walked out on her husband and her child. There was one possible explanation, and she made herself ask Adam, the day before she was to go home.

'Adam,' she said, with difficulty. 'This isn't easy to say, but — I must ask you this.'

He was completely still, waiting for her to speak, his grey eyes darkening.

'Adam — did I — have you any reason to think I might have gone off with — with someone else?'

She saw him relax, the tension leave his face and his eyes as he answered her.

'I don't think so, Christine,' he told her. 'I didn't think so at the time, there was no reason to think that that was why you had gone.' He looked away, not meeting her eyes. 'I can't say for certain, of course. At the time, I was so shattered that I couldn't think clearly, and I may have been wrong.' He smiled, the smile that lit up his face, and made him look again like the young Adam she had married. 'Anyway, neither the milkman nor the postman disappeared at the same time, so I think you can put that out of your mind.'

Christine smiled, trying to respond to his gentle teasing. But she didn't think the time would ever come when she could talk lightly of herself walking out on Adam and on Jenny.

She wanted Adam to bring Jenny to the hospital to see her, now that she knew the truth, but he wouldn't do it. He said that he thought it would be far better if she and Jenny met at home.

And when he came to take her home, he said something that made her stop brushing her hair, and turn round from the mirror, slowly, to look at him.

'You must realize, Christine,' he said, quietly, 'that it isn't going to be easy with Jenny.'

'What do you mean?' she asked, not understanding.

He hesitated.

'Ten years ago, when you — left,' he said, after a moment, 'Jenny was very upset at first. She — cried for you, most of the time. But gradually, as she grew older, she — changed.'

There was a hard ache in Christine's throat at the thought of Jenny, small and desperately unhappy, crying for the mother who had left her.

'How do you mean she changed?' she asked, with difficulty.

'She became — resentful, bitter, about you leaving us,' Adam said, after a moment. 'For many years now, she — hasn't mentioned you at all. Now — '

He hesitated, and Christine waited.

'Now,' he said at last, tiredly, 'I'm afraid her attitude is very much that having left us ten years ago, what right have you to come back now?'

Christine felt all the colour drain from her face.

'I'm sorry, Christine.' He took both her hands in his. 'Honey, I'm so sorry to have to say this to you. But I couldn't let you go home not knowing how Jenny feels.'

Christine shook her head, unable to say anything.

'And — you must see, honey, that it's reasonable for her to feel that way,' he pointed out.

'Yes, I can see that,' Christine replied, astonished at how steady her voice sounded. 'I — it was stupid of me not to have thought of that, wasn't it, Adam?' She tried to smile. 'Do you — do you think she'll change, after I'm home?'

He looked at her, gravely.

'I certainly hope so,' he said at last, and the lack of conviction in his voice shook her more than ever.

On the way home, he pointed out to her various changes, new buildings, new skylines in the once-familiar Edinburgh.

'Castle Rock hasn't changed,' she murmured, forcing her mind away from the thought of Jenny, the thought of what awaited her at home. 'And Prince's Street is still much the same. But surely that block is new?'

And as she looked around her, a realization came to her, not suddenly, but gradually.

'It's a long, long time since I've been in Edinburgh,' she said, and she saw Adam glance at her, quickly.

'Do you remember the last time?' he asked her, after a moment.

She thought about it, trying to pin down an elusive thought, more a feeling than a thought, that had come to her as she looked at the familiar outline of the Castle.

'No,' she said, regretfully. 'No, I don't remember anything, I just know that it's a long time since I was here.'

Expertly, Adam swung the big powerful car around the corner, and up towards Jenner Street. As he drew up at the house, Christine looked around her, wonderingly. The houses here were so much bigger than their little cottage in

Arthur's Crescent.

'You must be a very successful lawyer, Adam,' she said, suddenly reluctant to get out of the car.

He smiled.

'I am — I'm a member of the Council as well. A lot can happen in ten years, you know.'

Perhaps it can, Christine thought, forlornly, with a sudden ache of longing for the small house she rememberd, with the old apple tree on the lawn.

Two golden labradors came running across the grass, and she bent to greet them, glad of something to do, suddenly, traitorously wishing for the safety and impersonality of her hospital room.

'What are their names?' she asked Adam, her face buried in the golden fur.

'Not very original,' he told her, smiling. 'Guy and Doll.'

She looked up at him.

'What happened to old Mac?' she asked.

'He died — soon after you went away.'

It was a young voice, clear and cool. Christine stood up, and looked at her daughter.

She was tall and slim — taller than Christine herself. Her fair hair, thick and heavy like Adam's, swung in a golden curtain over her shoulders. The freckles had gone, and somehow her nose didn't seem to be snub any more. The Jenny Christine remembered, had had laughter in her eyes, and the corners of her mouth always looked as if a smile was there. This Jenny was a lovely girl — far lovelier than Christine would have guessed her funny little Jenny could turn out to be. But there was no warmth in her eyes, and her mouth was sullen, resentful.

'Jenny — oh, Jenny,' Christine said, unsteadily, and she held out her arms.

Jenny ignored her, and turned to her father.

'Aunt Valerie phoned to say she'll be over right away,' she told him. 'She has everything ready, but she had to go to town.'

'Jenny,' Adam's voice was hard, angry. 'Remember what I said. Your mother has been ill. I didn't hear you welcome her home.'

The girl looked at her father for a moment, and then, obviously not going as far as to defy him, she said, sullenly,

'Welcome home.'

Not Mummy, as she always used to say, Christine thought with sadness. Not even Mum or Mother. And yet — what more could she expect?

'Jenny,' Adam said, warningly.

She put her hand on his arm.

'Leave her, Adam,' she said, quietly. 'It — it can't be easy for her.' With an effort, she smiled. 'Aren't you going to show me this lovely house, Adam?'

Jenny knelt down to talk to the dogs, as Adam led Christine into the house. And Christine forced herself not to look back, all too conscious of the slim girl in her blue jeans and her striped top, with her back to the house, ignoring her mother.

It was a beautiful house, perfectly furnished. The sitting room was big and airy, and although it was warm for September, there was a fire glowing in the hearth, reflecting on the warm yellow and gold chintzes of the furniture and the curtains.

Christine touched the fireplace, smiling.

'I see you got your Adam fireplace,' she said. 'You always wanted one.'

'It seemed so right for me to have one,' he returned, smiling too.

Christine looked around the room, curiously. Much of it reflected the excellent taste Adam had always had, and hadn't been able to indulge in these early years of their marriage. But there was more than Adam's touch here.

'Who helped you to furnish and decorate the house, Adam?' she asked him.

He bent down to the coffee table,

moving a small porcelain horse.

'Valerie did,' he said, briefly. His eyes met hers. 'I had to move out of the other house, Christine. It held too many memories, and besides, it was too small. I have to do a fair bit of entertaining, you know.'

'I suppose so,' Christine agreed, levelly, remembering the entertaining they had done in the small house, in the early years when Jenny was a baby. Crowds of people — young people like themselves, with not much money, not much expensive furniture — sitting on the floor on cushions, talking, laughing, sometimes dancing. And a huge casserole of spaghetti or risotto, something cheap and filling. She looked around the quiet and beautiful room, seeing all too clearly that nowadays Adam's entertaining must be very different.

Adam looked at her, as if he wanted to say something, but through the window they both saw the small car draw up at the front door.

'Must be Valerie,' Adam said, and

there was relief in his voice, in the way he strode across the room and opened the door.

'Come on, Valerie — we're in here,' he called.

Valerie hadn't changed. Ten years ago she had been slim, dark and elegant, and she was still the same. She hurried forward and kissed Christine, her lips cool.

'I'm sorry I wasn't here when you arrived, Christine,' she said, warmly. She hesitated, and looked at Adam. 'How was Jenny?' she asked.

'Just as we expected,' Adam returned. 'I think I'll have to have a word with her.'

'I think you should,' Valerie agreed.

'Please — leave her alone,' Christine said, surprising herself. 'Give her time to get used to — to having me around.' She tried to smile, tried to hide her sudden annoyance at the swift exchanged glance between Adam and Valerie, 'She won't keep this up long. She's always been so sunny-natured.'

Again there was the swift exchange of glances.

'I'm afraid ten years have made quite a difference,' Valerie said, softly. 'Jenny — isn't quite as you remember her.' She smiled, sympathetically. 'It must be terribly hard for you, Christine, but you must understand how changed she is. She's seventeen, you know — not an easy age in any case. And of course — '

She paused, but there was no point in not going on, and Christine finished for her.

'And of course she's had a very difficult time, with her mother leaving her ten years ago?' she said. 'Isn't that what you were going to say, Valerie?'

Valerie shrugged.

'There's no point in denying the effect it has had on her,' she agreed. 'Let's have some tea.'

She pressed a bell that Christine hadn't seen, and almost immediately a middle-aged woman in a black dress and a white apron, came in with a tea-trolley.

'Shall I call Miss Jenny, Mr Lawrence?' she asked.

'No — leave her,' Christine said quickly. The woman looked at her, and there was such hostility in her glance that colour flooded Christine's cheeks.

'Mrs Howard, this is my wife,' Adam said pleasantly. 'Christine — Mrs Howard, who has been invaluable to me for quite a few years.'

The woman nodded, slightly, and murmured something before she turned and went out. Christine told herself that she just hadn't seen her out-stretched hand.

It was an awkward, strained half hour, in spite of Valerie's easy and friendly conversation. Everything was so strange to Christine — strange and somehow frightening, because it had changed so much. She couldn't hide her relief when Valerie suggested that she should lie down for a while and rest.

'Don't you think you should ring the office, Adam?' Valerie asked. 'You've been neglecting it dreadfully recently, you know, and I'm sure all sorts of things have cropped up. I'll take Christine upstairs.'

Easily, casually, she linked her arm through Christine's and led her up the wide and sweeping staircase.

'You've got a lovely view right across to the Firth from here,' she said lightly, opening a door. It was a single room, and suddenly, inexplicably, a wave of relief swept over Christine. 'Adam thought you'd like this room — it's quiet and peaceful, the rooms on the other side are too near the traffic. And you must still need lots of rest. His room and Jenny's are on the other side.'

That was all. She was right, of course, and it was what Christine wanted, but yet she couldn't suppress a slight resentment at the thought of Valerie and Adam discussing whether she should have her own room or whether she should share Adam's.

But what else could they do, Christine asked herself, reasonably. The question had to be decided, and just as obviously Valerie, who must have been a great help to Adam and to Jenny in these difficult years, was the person Adam would discuss it with.

Valerie opened the wardrobe.

'I bought you a few things,' she said casually. 'Just enough to be going on with. I hope they fit.' She smiled. 'Adam told me you were thinner than you used to be, and you certainly are. At least these slacks and jerseys should fit — we can do some shopping as soon as you feel up to it.'

She turned back the cover.

'Do rest now, Christine — you look exhausted, it must have been a very trying day. I'll see you later — I'm staying for dinner.' She hesitated. 'As a matter of fact, Adam asked me to move in for a few weeks, just until you're on your feet and can cope with things.'

'That's very kind of you, Valerie,' Christine replied, politely, 'but it's a lot of trouble.'

'Not at all,' Valerie assured her. 'I have this little boutique just off Prince's

Street, but I don't have to be there myself very often. And — ' She hesitated. 'So far, we've managed to keep any news of this out of the papers, Christine. Adam would rather nothing was said.'

Christine sat down on the bed, waves of exhaustion sweeping over her.

'That can't be easy, surely,' she said, evenly. 'I mean — how can Adam explain — suddenly having a wife again, after all these years?'

Valerie shrugged.

'He's still working that out,' she said, so lightly and easily that Christine told herself it was ridiculous to take offence. 'You must realize that he's very much in the public eye now, and he has to think of the best way to do this. Anyway, it's obviously going to be a little while before you're doing much, so there's time to think about it.'

Christine looked at her, surprised.

'What about Mrs Howard?' she asked. 'Surely she'll tell someone?'

'Not if Adam asks her not to,' Valerie

returned, with assurance. She smiled. 'Don't worry about it, Christine — it's just a question of finding the right time and the right way. Lie down and have a rest, I really feel worried about you, I'm sure you could have done with a little longer in hospital.'

Christine lay down, but just as she closed her eyes, she thought of something.

'What about the nurses?' she asked, foggily. 'Won't some of them tell people?'

'I doubt it,' Valerie replied. 'Adam has a fair bit of pull, you know, in various ways.' She went to the window and drew the curtains. 'Please don't worry about it, Christine — I just thought it was only fair that you should know.'

When she had gone, Christine lay still, forcing herself to relax. But in spite of her tiredness she was on edge, tense, and it was a long time before she fell asleep. Outside, she could hear the low murmur of Valerie's voice and Jenny's, and once she heard Jenny laugh. The easy tears of fatigue came to her eyes then, and she brushed them away impatiently, telling herself that she could expect nothing more, that Adam had warned her it wouldn't be easy with Jenny.

She slept then, but it was an uneasy sleep, full of strange, half-formed dreams. Sometimes she thought she was back in the hospital, struggling to tell the doctor and the nurses who she was, and where she lived. Sometimes she thought she was in the park, looking for Jenny, calling her name.

And then it seemed to her that she was walking along a road, tired, but determined to go on, putting one foot after the other, knowing only that she had to go on. Then she turned a corner, and there was a man ahead of her. Her heart lifted, for she knew that this was why she had been coming along this road. She began to run after him, and she tried to call, to ask him to wait, but she couldn't say anything. He kept on walking on, steadily, and she kept hurrying after him, trying to catch up with him. Then she stumbled, and when she looked up, he had gone.

She woke then, her heart thudding unevenly, her forehead wet with sweat. And suddenly it was more than she could bear, to go down into that big dining-room and sit at the table with Adam and Valerie and Jenny.

'Do you mind if I don't come down, Valerie?' she said, apologetically, when Valerie came in. 'I — I'm more tired than I thought I would be. Would it be too much trouble if I just had something on a tray here?'

'Of course not,' Valerie replied, warmly. 'You must just say what you want all the time, Christine, this is your home after all.'

Is it, Christine thought sadly when Valerie had gone. It didn't feel like her home. It was a beautiful house, which belonged to her husband. Presumably Jenny had grown up here, for Adam had said he had moved about eight years ago. And yet it seemed to Christine that it was a shell of a house, with no warmth and no easiness about it. She told herself how ridiculous it was to feel like that, and yet once the feeling was admitted, there was no hiding it.

Slowly, her days began to fall into a pattern. She had breakfast in bed, brought to her by the housekeeper, Mrs Howard. Soon after that she dressed and went downstairs. There was a small morning-room, less perfect and less intimidating than the sitting-room, and she usually sat there. As soon as it was warm enough — and although it was late in the year, there was an Indian summer, with day after day of golden and warm autumn weather — she went outside, to walk around the garden, or to sit in the sunshine, a book or a magazine lying on her lap.

Valerie was usually there, although sometimes she spent a few hours in her boutique. And Jenny was often there, when she didn't feel like going to lectures at the Art College.

'You used to say you wanted to be a nurse, Jenny,' Christine said to her one day, walking across to the garage door where Jenny was grooming the two dogs.

'Did I?' Jenny replied, without much interest. 'I don't remember.'

But I remember, her mother thought sadly. I remember a little girl with all her dolls lined up to make a hospital, and a white apron I had made for her with a red cross on it, and a little hat.

'Don't you remember the nurse's uniform I made for you, Jenny?' she asked wistfully.

'No,' Jenny replied briefly, rudely.

Christine flushed at the hostility in her voice and in the set of her shoulders.

'Don't you remember when your doll Anna-Marie fell out of the window, and you bandaged her and you said her leg was broken?' she asked.

Jenny shook her head. Then, unexpectedly, she looked up.

'I only remember one thing,' she

said, in a small cool voice. 'I remember that you walked out and left us ten years ago, without a word.'

She stood up and whistled to the dogs, and then she walked away without a backward glance.

Christine stood watching her, all the colour drained from her face.

She didn't want to say anything about it to Adam, especially when Valerie was there, which she so often was. Then one evening Valerie was out at a concert, and Christine and Adam had dinner alone, for Jenny was out as well.

'Have some more steak, Christine,' Adam urged. 'You have a long way to go — you haven't anything like the colour in your cheeks that you should have.'

Christine shook her head.

'I'm not hungry, thank you, Adam.' She hesitated. 'Where is Jenny? She — she didn't say where she was going.'

Adam looked at her quickly.

'She's at some college hop with one

of her bearded boy-friends,' he told her lightly. He hesitated, and then went on, quietly, 'Christine — it isn't getting any easier with Jenny, is it?'

Christine shook her head, the familiar ache in her throat.

'I didn't realize she would go on feeling like this,' she murmured. Then, all at once desperate, she looked across the table at him. 'Adam — I've been thinking. Maybe it would be better if I — if I went away?'

He was still, watching her.

'Why should you do that, honey?' he asked her, and the gentleness of his voice brought treacherous tears to her eyes.

She shook her head, desolate.

'It isn't doing much good, being here,' she murmured. 'Jenny doesn't want me.'

It was a long time before he spoke. Too long, she thought, afterwards.

'It isn't only Jenny, Christine,' he pointed out, quietly. 'I want you.'

She shook her head.

71

'I've been away too long,' she said. 'You and Jenny — you've got used to being without me, you've made your lives without me.'

'Where would you go?' he asked her. 'You're still far from well, honey.'

Back to where I came from, Christine thought with sudden, shattering certainty. If only I knew where that was.

'I don't know,' she admitted.

Adam smiled.

'Let's have no more nonsense about going, then,' he said cheerfully. And then, seriously, 'Christine — we must all expect that it isn't going to be easy. We can't just take up where we left off ten years ago, you know.'

'I know that,' Christine agreed quietly, thinking of Jenny's sullen rudeness, thinking of the little girl she remembered. There seemed to be nothing of her Jenny in this girl.

And yet, sometimes, there was a glimpse.

One morning Christine looked out of her window and saw Jenny playing on the grass with the dogs, throwing the ball for them to bring back to her. The bigger dog, Guy, brought her the ball and then lay on his back, his big paws waving in the air, the ball still between his teeth.

'You big silly,' Jenny said, laughing, pretending to take the ball from him. He growled, and she laughed again. 'You don't convince me,' she told him, 'not when your tail's wagging like that. Come on, give it to me.'

She took it from him, and he jumped at her, knocking her over, so that girl and dog fell together, Jenny laughing. Christine, watching, had a swift, stabbing glimpse of the small Jenny she remembered, with the surprisingly deep laugh, and her eyes bright and unclouded. She leaned out of the window, all the breath gone from her body with the depth of this emotion sweeping through her. Come back to me, Jenny, she said, silently. Come back to me the way you used to be when you were my little girl.

Then Jenny looked up and saw her.

All the laughter died from her face, all the warmth from her eyes. Without saying anything, she turned away, the thick silken curtain of hair swinging over her face.

'Jenny,' Christine called, impulsively.

But Jenny didn't turn around.

Defeated, Christine drew her head in and closed the window.

The last hint of autumn had gone now, and early in November the weather became cold and misty, so that even to walk in the garden was chilly. Valerie had to spend some time at her boutique.

'I hate leaving you alone like this, Christine,' she said worriedly one morning just before she left.

'I'm all right,' Christine replied, politely. And she told herself that she mustn't let Valerie see that in fact she'd rather be on her own. Valerie had been so kind, giving up so much of her time to come here, it seemed ungrateful, but yet Christine knew, with an instinct that went deeper than any reasoning, that between Valerie and her there was a reservation.

'What will you do?' Valerie asked as Christine went out with her to her car.

Christine shrugged.

'Read, probably.'

'You read most of yesterday morning,' Valerie pointed out, lightly, 'Would you like me to bring you some wool so that you can knit?'

It seemed churlish to refuse, so Christine agreed. She found a pattern in a magazine of a skinny rib sweater just right for Jenny, and the next day she started it. Mrs Howard had lit the fire in the little morning-room, and she sat there. The wool was fine, a soft lilac shade, and she thought that it would suit Jenny. If Jenny would be prepared to accept something her mother had done for her. But in spite of her doubts, there was something pleasant and satisfying about knitting for Jenny, and she watched with satisfaction as the fine lilac rib grew.

And then, quite suddenly, her hands

grew still, and she looked at the knitting in her hands, confused. There was something wrong. Why was she knitting something so soft and fine, instead of the thick navy or blue she usually knitted?

Christine's breath caught in her throat.

But the elusive thought had gone, leaving nothing for her to grasp, to get a hold of. She looked at her knitting again, but now it was nothing more nor less than the sweater she was knitting for Jenny.

That evening, as they sat at the fire, Valerie suggested that they should have a party, to let people know that Christine had come back.

'After all,' she pointed out, reasonably, 'sooner or later people must know. This way, we tell a few people quietly, explain that Christine hasn't been well enough until now. Then, after the party, these people will spread the news, and that's all there is to it. With luck we'll keep it out of the papers — either you or I know most of the big boys there.'

'I suppose so,' Adam agreed, reluctantly. He turned to Christine. 'Feel you could stand up to a party, honey?'

'No, not yet, please, Adam,' Christine said quickly, panic sweeping over her at the thought of facing a lot of strange people, of having them wonder about these ten missing years.

But Adam didn't give up so easily. Later, when she had gone to bed, he came up.

'Try to see it my way, honey,' he pointed out, reasonably. He smiled, and again the smile didn't reach his eyes. 'You can't deny that it puts a man in an awkward position when his wife suddenly reappears after ten years. Valerie is right, something must be said, and soon. After all, you want to be able to move around freely, don't you?'

'Who would be coming?' Christine asked reluctantly. 'Just — just people we know — people we knew well? Like Marge and Jim, and Betty and Duncan? I wouldn't mind that, Adam.'

He shrugged.

'I hadn't thought of them,' he said, carelessly. 'Actually, I haven't seen much of any of that crowd for years. You know how it is.'

No, Christine thought sadly. No, Adam, I don't know how it is, I'm afraid.

'No, we — I had thought more of a few business connections, some other members of the council — that sort of thing. Just some of the people I mix with a fair bit.'

She was too tired to argue any more.

'All right,' she agreed, quietly. 'If you want, Adam.'

'Fine,' he said, enthusiastically. 'I'll get Valerie to arrange everything.'

When he had gone, Christine slept, the sleep of complete exhaustion. In the first moment of waking, she knew that someone was in the room with her. She opened her eyes, and saw Jenny there. And just for a moment, there was a softness in the girl's face, almost a warmth. Then it was gone, and the sulleness and coldness were back, so that Christine wondered if she had just imagined the way Jenny had looked.

'Hello, Jenny,' she murmured, drowsily.

'Are you all right?' Jenny asked, abruptly. 'You've been asleep for ages.'

'I was tired out,' Christine confessed. 'I didn't realize just how little I can do without getting tired.' She hesitated. 'I — I went to see the old house, Jenny.'

The girl was silent, and Christine went on, with difficulty.

'I wanted to see it, but it had changed so much.'

Jenny looked at her, curiously.

'Is it really true that you don't remember anything about — about going away and leaving us, or about these ten years?' she asked.

Christine nodded, conscious of a pulse beating in her throat. This was the first time Jenny had actually talked to her.

'I'm afraid it is,' she said, steadily. 'It — isn't very pleasant, not knowing where you've been or what you've been doing.'

Abruptly, as if feeling she had unbent too much, the girl rose. When she was at the door, Christine asked her quickly if she would be in that evening.

Jenny shook her head.

'No, I'm going out.' She hesitated, and then, abruptly, went on. 'His name is Clive Burnett — he's an art student too.'

Then she went out. Christine lay back against her pillows, smiling a little. It hadn't been much, but — it was a beginning.

She got up and dressed, then. Valerie was sitting at the small desk writing, abstracted. She looked up when Christine went in.

'Hello,' she said, smiling. 'You look rested. I'm just making lists for Adam. She looked out of the window, and shivered. 'Look at that fog now.'

As she said it, there was the sound of a ship's siren from the distant Firth. A long and mournful sound. And yet, hearing it, Christine's heart leapt joyfully. There was a moment of pure happiness, and then, as suddenly as it had come, it was gone. And she had no idea why it had been there, no memory of why the sound of a ship's siren should have made her feel like that.

But that night, she dreamed again.

She dreamed that she was on the same road, walking after the same man, and slowly, gradually, gaining on him. She kept her eyes fixed on him, knowing that she mustn't lose sight of him.

The road was in shadow, but suddenly he moved out into bright sunlight and turned towards her, but the sunlight blinded her so that she couldn't see him.

'Chris!' he called, joyfully, and she began to run towards him.

Then, suddenly, she reached him and she saw that he was Adam. But she knew that it hadn't been Adam she was running to, that it hadn't been Adam who called to her.

She woke then, and she was weeping. Weeping, she realized with a heavy feeling of loss, for a man whose name she didn't know, for a man whose face she couldn't even remember.

3

Christine tried to tell herself that it was only a dream, that it meant nothing.

But she knew, with a certainty that defied logic and reasoning, that somewhere there was a man she had loved deeply. And she was certain, too, that this was why there was a barrier between Adam and her, why she felt herself shrinking from him when he touched her.

And in spite of what Adam had said when she asked him in the hospital, she wondered, more and more, whether she had known this man ten years ago, whether she had left Adam to go to him.

If I ever remember, she thought with sadness and acceptance one day, I will go to him and tell him that — whatever there was between us must be over. I have come back to Adam — something made me come back to him, made me forget these ten years as if they never happened — and because of that, because of the way I hurt him all these years ago, I can't hurt him again.

Valerie was preparing for the Saturday night party, efficiently and competently telephoning people, organizing food, drinks, on such a scale that Christine's heart sank.

'You must have done this a fair bit for Adam?' she said one morning, questioning.

'Yes, I have,' Valerie replied without looking up. Then she put down her pen on the list she was making, carefully, and looked across at Christine.

'Christine — don't you remember? I used to help with this sort of thing even before you — went away? When you felt the entertaining Adam wanted to do was getting beyond you?'

Christine looked at her, fear closing up her throat, for she remembered nothing of this.

She shook her head.

'What do you remember?' Valerie asked, quite gently. 'About me, for example?'

Christine folded her hands together and stared down at the dull gold of her wedding ring.

'You came back,' she said, slowly. 'You'd been away, in America — you went soon after Adam and I were married. Then you came back — just before Jenny's seventh birthday. Not long before — before I went away.' With difficulty, she met Valerie's eyes. 'I — don't remember you helping with entertaining, Valerie, I'm sorry.'

The other woman looked at her, thoughtfully.

'How soon after Jenny's birthday would you say you went away?'

'I don't know — how can I, when I don't remember?' Christine replied quickly, the now-familiar fear paralysing her, the fear of this gap in her life.

'But that day in the park — when you came back — you must have had some feeling about her age, some thought?'

Valerie asked, quietly, insistently.

Christine closed her eyes, fighting the panic, trying to think of that day.

'I knew she was seven,' she said at last, slowly. 'I — I think that I thought it wasn't long after her birthday. I'm not sure why, but I think so.' A fragment of a memory came back to her from the early days in the hospital, the time soon after Adam had come. 'I remember thinking what a good thing it was that you were back from America, to look after Jenny.'

For a moment, Valerie's hand touched hers, sympathetically.

'In fact, Christine,' she said clearly, 'I had been back from America for almost a year when you went away. Jenny was very nearly eight.'

Bewildered, Christine looked at her.

'But why don't I remember that?' she asked, her voice low. 'Why don't I remember up to the time I went away? I — I thought that I did, I thought it was only the actual going away that I had forgotten.'

'You mustn't worry about it,' Valerie said, obviously concerned. 'I shouldn't have said anything.'

Christine shook her head.

'It's all right,' she replied, hardly knowing what she was saying. Because it did worry her, to have this new factor thrown in, this realization that the gap in her memory was even longer, even more inexplicable than she had thought. To have forgotten from the moment she walked out on Adam — there was something vaguely understandable about that. Thinking about it, as she so often did, she had decided that in some way her mind had blanked out from that moment, because she was so ashamed of what she had done. But this — to know that as well as that there was a whole section of that last year before she went that she had forgotten as well —

She stood up, restless, trying to control herself, trying to think of something else.

'Isn't there something I can do to help for Saturday, Valerie?' she asked. 'I feel so useless sitting around when you're so busy.'

Valerie looked at the list in her hand.

'I have to go over to the boutique for a couple of hours,' she said. 'Could you check through this list of food, see what we have, and what we still need?' She led the way through to the kitchen, where Mrs Howard was baking. 'Mrs Lawrence is going to check these things for us, Mrs Howard,' she said easily. 'Christine, lay out on this shelf what we have, and tick on the list what we still need, will you? That will be such a help to me.'

When she had gone, Christine began checking the list, a little awkwardly, all too conscious of Mrs Howard in the room with her. She tried to talk, but the older woman was so uncommunicative that eventually she gave up, and concentrated on her work. It didn't take long, and she was almost sorry when she had finished. The rest of the morning stretched out ahead of her now. She set the list with its ticks beside the neat rows of tins she had found, and then she went back through to the morning-room and her knitting. Later, she took the two dogs out for a walk, holding their leads firmly, for they were young dogs, and boisterous. Old Mac hadn't even needed a lead, when they took him out.

Jenny came home first, and Christine told her that she had taken the dogs out.

'Thanks,' Jenny replied, ungraciously, standing as she always did when talking to her mother, as if poised for instant flight. 'I hope you remembered to close the gate — neither of them have any traffic sense.'

Christine forced herself not to be hurt.

'I know it's always kept closed,' she replied, quietly. 'You — you don't mind if I take them out sometimes? It gives me something to do.'

Jenny shrugged.

'I don't mind,' she replied. 'As long as you close the gate, and see that they

89

can't get on to the road.'

She went out, then, and Christine went back to her knitting. She hadn't said to Jenny that she was knitting something for her, and the girl had never asked. When it's finished, Christine told herself, I'll just give it to her.

She heard Valerie's car, soon after that, but Valerie must have gone through to the kitchen, for it was a while before she came through, and just as she did Adam came as well, and they went to have lunch. Once or twice, Christine looked up to find Valerie looking at her, and there was something in the other woman's eyes that made her uncomfortable. But it was only when they were all sitting having coffee that Valerie spoke directly to her:

'I'm sorry you felt too tired to check the tins, Christine,' she said, gently. 'Just give me the list and I'll do it now.'

Christine looked at her, bewildered.

'But I did check them,' she replied, surprised. 'I set them on the lower shelf and I ticked the things we still needed on the list.'

There was a swiftly-exchanged glance between Adam and Valerie, and then Adam said, soothingly, that it wasn't worth bothering about, it wouldn't take Valerie long in any case.

'But I did do it,' Christine protested, close to tears. 'Come with me, Valerie, and I'll show you.'

Adam and Valerie, followed her, both with obvious reluctance. Mrs Howard was sitting at the kitchen table, drinking a cup of tea and reading the morning paper.

'Don't get up, Mrs Howard,' Valerie said easily. 'We won't be a minute.'

Christine opened the larder door.

But the shelf was empty. The tins she had laid out had gone. Bewildered, she looked at the other shelves, and there they were, back where she had first seen them.

She turned to Valerie, meeting the other woman's pitying glance.

'I did do it,' she said, shakily. 'Look

— there's the list on the floor, you can see where I — '

Her voice trailed off.

For it was the list, in Valerie's unmistakable slanted hand-writing. But there were no ticks on it.

'Christine — for heavens' sake forget it, it doesn't matter,' Adam said, and she could hear the mild exasperation in his voice.

'It does matter,' Christine told him, stubbornly. She turned to Mrs Howard. 'Mrs Howard — you were here, you saw me checking these tins. Has — has anyone moved them'

The older woman shook her head.

'I'm sorry, Mrs Lawrence,' she replied, her face smooth, impassive. 'I've been in here most of the morning, and you've been in the morning-room, knitting. I brought you in some tea about eleven — remember?'

'Of course I remember,' Christine replied, impatiently. 'But before that, I came in here — I spoke to you.'

'I'm sorry, Mrs Lawrence,' the

housekeeper said again.

'I think you're over-tired, honey,' Adam told her lightly — too lightly. 'Come and lie down for a bit.'

She shook his arm off her shoulder.

'I'm not over-tired, Adam,' she said, trying to speak evenly, 'and I know I did these tins. Someone — someone must have moved them.'

'Of course they must have, Christine dear,' Valerie put in quickly. 'That's what must have happened, Adam, isn't it? Isn't it, Adam?'

'Of course,' Adam replied after a moment — a moment in which Christine was all too conscious of Valerie's dark eyes telling Adam to agree with her.

There was nothing else she could say. Tiredly, she turned away, and went up to her room.

I did do the tins, she told herself fiercely. And then, remembering the empty shelf, the list without any of the ticks she had been so certain she would find, remembering the housekeeper's statement that she hadn't come into the kitchen — she began to feel doubtful. If I can forget ten years, she thought, worried, uncertain, I could forget what I did today. Or what I thought I did.

Neither Adam nor Valerie mentioned the small incident again, and Christine couldn't bring herself to. It seemed better to put it out of her mind, to try to forget it completely, to put it down to over-tiredness, as Valerie had said.

And yet, Christine thought with a flash of rebellion, why should I be over-tired? Except of doing nothing.

The household seemed to run smoothly, with the ease of many years of practise. Mrs Howard needed no supervision, and although she seemed to have no objection when Valerie discussed any arrangements with her, Christine was quite sure that she wouldn't take the same thing well from herself. The arrangements for the party went on smoothly, and on the Saturday morning Valerie took Christine to have her hair done, and to choose a terrace dress at the boutique.

'This is the one I thought of for you,' Valerie said, giving Christine a dress of shot silk, in glowing oranges and browns. Christine put it on, wishing the girl at the hairdresser's had done her hair less elaborately, more casually.

'Just right — I thought it would be,' Valerie said, pleased, zipping the back of the dress.

Christine looked at the woman in the mirror, slim and elegant, her brown hair swept smoothly back and up.

'Heavens,' she said, laughing, 'I don't know how long it is since I wore anything like this.'

In the mirror, Valerie's eyes met hers, and her laughter died away. She didn't know what had made her say it, and yet she knew it was true. This dress, and the woman in the mirror, didn't fit with the life she had known, she was completely certain of that.

'How do you know that?' Valerie asked, quietly.

'I don't know — I just know it,'

Christine told her honestly. She hesitated. 'It — it's like fishing, Valerie. Like sitting for hours waiting, and then suddenly there's something on the line, and I've drawn it up without thinking, without knowing what it's going to be.'

'That's a funny thing to say,' Valerie said. 'What on earth makes you think of fishing? You've never fished in your life.'

'Never fished?' Christine replied, surprised. 'I've spent hours fishing, I love fishing — "

Her voice trailed away under Valerie's steady gaze.

'I know I love fishing,' she said, shakily. 'I — I don't know where or when I learned to fish, but — I know I've done a lot of fishing.'

She turned away and unzipped the dress, stepping out of it.

'Do you want this one?' Valerie asked.

Christine nodded.

'Yes, thank you.' And then, because Valerie had gone to so much trouble for her — 'It's a lovely dress, Valerie, I'll enjoy wearing it. And — thanks for taking me to have my hair done too.'

Neither she nor Valerie said much to each other on the way home, and Christine was glad of the busy party preparations which kept Valerie very much occupied for the rest of the day.

When Christine came down, dressed, Jenny was in the room, wearing a long white dress that showed off her golden tan.

'You do look nice, Jenny,' Christine told her impulsively.

Jenny flushed.

'I'd rather be wearing my jeans,' she said, defensively. 'But Aunt Valerie and Daddy said I had to dress up. And — Clive's coming. He hates dressing up too, but if we're together it won't be so bad.'

Her face lit up when she talked of this Clive, Christine realized. She hesitated, wanting to ask Jenny about him, but afraid of making Jenny retreat again. Instead, she said casually that Jenny's tan was lovely.

'We had a holiday in Switzerland not

so long ago,' Jenny told her.

We? Christine wondered who we were.

'Daddy and Aunt Valerie and me,' the girl volunteered. 'It was — it was just before you — came back.'

This was dangerous ground, and yet Christine was reluctant to let Jenny go, although she could see that the girl was impatient now.

'Do you like my dress, Jenny?' she asked. 'Aunt Valerie chose it for me.'

'It suits you,' Jenny said after a moment. 'But I like your hair better when you do it yourself. It looks more like — '

She stopped. Christine waited, afraid to say anything, afraid almost to breathe.

'More like it was before you went away,' the girl finished, abruptly. Then, as if afraid she had said too much, she turned and ran out.

The boy, Clive, was the first to arrive. Jenny brought him in, casual, a little defensive, both of them looking uncomfortable. Valerie and Adam were there as well, and Clive greeted them easily, obviously having met them both before.

'This is my mother, Clive,' Jenny introduced them, awkwardly. 'Clive Burnett.'

Christine shook hands with the boy, thinking sadly that Jenny still couldn't bring herself to say Mum or even Mother.

'Pleased to meet you, Mrs Lawrence. Gee — it's quite something you turning up out of the blue like this, isn't it?' he said eagerly.

'I suppose it is,' Christine agreed, amused and suddenly at home with this boy, in spite of his beard and his long hair. There was no pretence here, no careful skating over thin ice — he was honest, like all the boys she'd known.

The thought brought her up short, the thought and the knowledge, the conviction that she had known many boys, known them well, that in fact she was more at ease with teenage boys than she was with her own teenage daughter. She knew that she had a background of experience with boys of this age, a background that came from some forgotten time in some forgotten place.

But there was no more time to think of this, for the guests were arriving, and there was a bewildering array of faces and names, of people shaking hands with her and murmuring, awkwardly, how wonderful it was that she was there. Politely, Christine shook hands and listened to Adam's introductions, and then, when most people seemed to have arrived, and there were small groups of people standing around the big room talking and drinking, she retreated, thankfully, to the big bay window, sipping her drink, wishing she could get out of here.

Just then, across the crowded room, she saw an elderly man arrive. He was a small man, with bright blue eyes under bristling white eyebrows. But I know him, she thought, surprised, and she thought that there was a moment of recognition in the vivid blue eyes as he looked at her across the room. And then the elusive thread of recollection had gone, and he was just an elderly guest at Adam's cocktail party, a guest whom Adam introduced as John Scott, editor of the Evening Star. Then someone else claimed Mr Scott's attention, and he had to turn away.

But he didn't say anything, Christine told herself. And — and even if he did recognize me, perhaps we knew him ten years ago, Adam and I.

She had no recollection of this, though, no tie-up of this man with her life with Adam in the little cottage. And somehow, as the evening drew on, as the guests moved from group to group, talking, laughing, as she met more and more strange people who looked at her with barely-hidden curiousity, she felt more and more certain that if she had been right about that moment of recognition, then it must be in the lost ten years that she had known this man.

It wasn't easy, for Christine, going up to him directly and speaking to him.

But something told her that she had to do it, had to take this chance.

At last she saw him standing alone, looking around him, and she went across to him, quickly, before she could lose her courage.

'Mr Scott,' she said, more loudly than she had meant to, and he turned to her smiling.

'Ah — my hostess,' he greeted her. 'I haven't had the pleasure of talking to you tonight, Mrs Lawrence — too many people wanting to meet Adam's beautiful wife.'

Christine flushed.

'Mr Scott,' she said, impulsively, 'Before I met you — when I saw you across the room, I had the feeling I'd known you somewhere.'

The older man rubbed his chin, his bright blue eyes studying her.

'Funny you should say that,' he replied, slowly. 'Just for a moment, across there, I did think I knew you. And then, when I looked at you properly, I knew I was wrong.'

Christine's heart sank.

'Why did you think you were wrong?' she asked, trying to speak casually, lightly.

He shrugged.

'Can't really say,' he told her, apologetically. 'The woman I was thinking of — she was just different, in many ways.' He smiled. 'It was just one of these fleeting mistakes — you know, you wave to someone and then you realize that you don't know them at all.'

'Where did you meet this woman?' Christine asked, knowing by the surprise on his face that her insistence was wrong, knowing she should have left the whole thing.

He laughed.

'Nowhere you'd be likely to know, Mrs Lawrence,' he told her, easily. 'It's a tiny fishing village on the West Coast — called Tormore. The kind of place no one has ever heard of, but I once spent a holiday there when I'd been ill. Years ago.'

Tormore. Tormore.

At last, regretfully, she had to admit that it meant nothing to her, that there was no sense of recognition in the sound of the word, that it was just a name.

The week after the party, she had to go back to the hospital for a checkup. She was glad to see Dr Ruthven again, glad of the friendly way he greeted her.

'Nothing wrong with your arm and your ribs,' he said at last, cheerfully. 'But you're still much too thin — you look as if a breath could blow you away. Still getting headaches?'

The abrupt question startled Christine, and she flushed.

'Yes, sometimes,' she admitted, with reluctance.

'I'm not surprised,' the doctor said. 'You were badly concussed.' He hesitated. 'Your husband tells me you sometimes have some confusion about whether you've done things or not.'

Christine felt all the colour drain from her face.

'I did, once,' she said slowly. 'But I — I still think there was some mistake about it.'

'Perhaps there was,' the doctor agreed. 'Don't worry, anyway — quite likely you could have some confusion over small things, after the time you've had. Any success in remembering anything about these ten years?'

Christine shook her head.

'Sometimes there are small things I remember. Like fishing.' She told him of her certainty that she enjoyed fishing and had done a fair amount of it, and she told him too of the feeling she had had that she wasn't accustomed to wearing smart clothes and being at parties. 'But it's just feelings,' she finished, wistfully, 'there's nothing really to go on.'

She said nothing about the dream, about the man she was trying so hard to catch up with, about her bitter disappointment when she saw that it was Adam, and not the other man, the one she had heard call her Chris.

She looked up at the doctor, distressed.

'It seems so awful,' she said, shakily, 'that I can just shut out ten years of my life like that. It's like — ' She paused trying to think what it was like, trying to clear the confusion of her own thoughts. 'It's as if I'd been living in one room of a house, and then I went into another and put the light on. And — and when I put that light on, the other light went off, so that the first room was dark.' She nodded at him, anxiously. 'Does that seem clear to you?'

He nodded.

'Clear enough.' He hesitated. 'But just occasionally there's a flash of light, and you do see something from the other room? Is that right?'

'Not really see it,' Christine admitted, slowly. 'Not clearly. Just enough to — to let me know there is something in that other room. More a feeling than really seeing anything.'

She thought of the moment when the

106

knitting she was doing had seemed strange to her, and she thought of hearing the ship's siren, and her instant happiness. But there was too little, really, in either of them even to mention to the doctor, and so she said nothing.

'Please keep in touch with us, Mrs Lawrence,' Dr Ruthven said then, rising. 'And — if anything worries you, if you have any more confusion, then I think we should have another look at you, perhaps in hospital.'

Christine looked at him, unable to say anything, a new fear growing.

'Don't worry, my dear.' He patted her shoulder. 'I'm sure this will clear itself up, but if not — there are quite a few things we could do to help you.'

Adam was waiting for her in the car, and she joined him, too shaken to say anything until at last, anxiously, he asked her if everything was all right.

'Yes, I'm all right,' Christine murmured. And then, unable to keep silent any longer, she burst out — 'Adam — why did you tell him about the tins, and — and me not remembering? You shouldn't have — there was no need to.'

For a moment his hand left the wheel and covered hers, but she drew back.

'I had to, Christine,' he said after a moment. 'It didn't seem right not to.'

Christine stared out of the window, her eyes blurred with tears.

'He — he thinks that if there's anything more like that, I should go back into hospital,' she told him, shakily.

'I'm sure there won't be,' Adam said comfortingly.

But she had the certainty that he was only saying it, that he didn't really believe there was no need to worry about her not remembering what she had done. And once or twice, in the following days, she found him looking at her, his grey eyes clouded, thoughtful. She waited for him to speak, but he said nothing.

I won't think about it, Christine told herself determinedly. It — it doesn't really matter, anyone has moments of

— of being absent-minded.

And she forced her mind away from the depressing and worrying thoughts, forced herself to think, instead, of Jenny.

For slowly, gradually, Jenny's antagonism seemed to be disappearing.

Sometimes when she came home from Art College, instead of going right up to her own room, she would come and look for her mother. Then, perched on the arm of a chair or the back of the couch, she would talk about what she had done. And about Clive. Most of all, she talked about Clive. Talked about him in an offhand, casual way that didn't deceive Christine at all.

Sometimes, although the November weather was cold, they took the dogs out together, Christine with one and Jenny with the other. Jenny's cheeks glowed with the cold, and her thick fair hair swung on her shoulders as they walked along briskly, and Christine, looking at her tall daughter, began to see more of her own small Jenny in the girl beside her.

'Am I going too fast for you, Mummy?' Jenny said one day, casually.

Christine's heart thudded against her ribs.

'No — I can manage,' she returned. 'You mustn't treat me like an invalid, Jenny, because I'm not.'

Jenny looked at her, critically.

'No,' she said after a moment, 'You're not. You're looking more and more like yourself all the time.'

Then she coloured, conscious of what she had said. Quickly, she began to talk of something else, and after a moment's disappointment, Christine followed suit. There must be no rushing Jenny, her confidence would have to be won so slowly, so carefully. But now Christine was beginning to hope that there really was a chance of this, where at first it had seemed impossible.

It seemed to her that Jenny was far less sullen and withdrawn than she had been, as well as less hostile. But thinking of this, Christine could see, with pain and with shame, what a dreadful thing she had done to Jenny, to the small seven-year-old Jenny, by leaving her. More and more, it seemed inconceivable to her that she had done this.

What saddened and bewildered her, was the way she felt about Adam. She was certain, looking back through the years, that she and Adam had been close, had been fond of each other. Had been in love with each other, she told herself. And yet, she knew with certainty that there was nothing of that left. And because of that knowledge, she wondered more and more about the man she had dreamed about, the man who had called her Chris, the man she had run to so joyously.

Had she known him ten years ago, had she loved him then? Had she loved him so much that she would leave her child because of him?

To Christine, this seemed impossible. However strong her feelings for this man had been, she was sure that she would not leave Jenny, sure that she wouldn't have gone away so deliberately and broken up her marriage. It didn't fit with everything that she felt instinctively — about marriage, and about Jenny.

And in some strange way, although she did not know this man's name, although she couldn't even remember his face, she knew that he too would regard marriage as a promise not to be lightly broken. How she knew this she couldn't tell, it was something she must have learned from some forgotten event, some forgotten exchange between them. But she knew.

And knowing this, she wondered sometimes if he felt the same aching sense of loss, of incompleteness, that she felt more and more. The day Jenny called her Mummy — there was a moment of delight, of wanting to share her joy with someone, before she realized that the person she wanted to share it with wasn't there — wouldn't ever be there again, for her.

Sometimes at night, when she couldn't sleep, she thought of him, and wondered where he was. If I ever remember, she promised silently once, tears of loneliness running down her cheeks, then I'll come to you and I'll tell you.

She didn't know, she realized forlornly, whether she had told him that she was going back to Adam, or whether she had just gone. In either case, she had left him.

After a sleepless night of thinking about the whole thing, it seemed to Christine that the only thing she could do — the only way of trying to put right the wrong she had done so long ago, was to accept that this man and this part of her life were over. The light in that room had gone out, it might never come on again. But the light was on in this room, this room that held her marriage to Adam, and her daughter. All she could do was to go on from here, to do her utmost to re-make her marriage.

But it wasn't going to be easy, there was no use deceiving herself. She found that at night, trying to sleep, everything in her mind would whirl, as she tried to see where she was going. I don't know where I've been, and — I don't really know where I'm going either, she thought confusedly.

And then, trying to be sensible, she told herself that she must sleep, must be able to face the next day clearly. She decided to go down to the kitchen and warm some milk.

The door of the small study was half open, and the light was on. Surprised that Adam was still up, for it was late, Christine went to the door. But before she could push it properly open, or say anything, she stopped.

'I don't like it, Adam,' Valerie was saying, worriedly. 'I don't like it at all.'

'Stop worrying,' Adam returned, lazily. 'I only told you so that you'd know how things are.' His voice was low now. 'Come here — this whole thing is driving me round the bend.'

'No, Adam — not here,' Valerie murmured.

And then she laughed, a low, soft laugh, a laugh meant to tease.

'Jenny's asleep and Christine's asleep,' Adam said then. 'Come here.'

There was a rough insistence in his voice that brought hot colour to Christine's cheeks.

Slowly, silently, she turned and went back upstairs, forgetting why she had come down, forgetting everything but this.

Adam — and Valerie.

4

Adam — and Valerie.

Now that she knew, it seemed to Christine that she had been very foolish not to have seen this before. They had been very careful — she could see that now, looking back, but — she could have guessed.

She sat down on her bed, still drowsy from the sleeping-pill, uncertain what she was going to do. It was natural, she told herself, reasonably, that Adam and Valerie should have fallen in love with each other, thrown together as they must have been over all these years she had been away. She couldn't blame them.

And even less could she blame them when she thought of the man she had dreamed about, the man she knew she would never stop missing and longing for. If she had loved someone else, why shouldn't Adam?

Yet she knew, with a lack of generosity which she had to admit to, that it would have bothered her less if it had been anyone but Valerie. For in spite of all Valerie's kindness and thoughtfulness, in spite of her help and her sympathy, Christine admitted now that she didn't like her. 'There was nothing she could put her finger on, nothing specific — only this instinctive dislike.

But I must be fair to Adam, Christine told herself. If Valerie is the one he loves, then that is the end of it. Or — or perhaps the beginning.

For she knew that she must set Adam free.

She must put right what she had done ten years ago by letting him find some happiness now with Valerie. She saw now, with sadness, that there was nothing left between Adam and her, nothing at all. All they had in common now was their daughter.

And because of Jenny, Christine

thought, I will not rush into this. I will give him his freedom, but — first I will think about it, about what it will mean to me, with regard to Jenny.

Now, with a new warmth and understanding growing between Jenny and herself, she was determined that nothing was going to spoil this. Jenny, she was certain, would blame Christine for any divorce, at this stage.

She thought about talking to Adam, about discussing it with him, but when she began to consider what she would say to him, how she would say it, she realized that in fact any discussion, any bringing into the open, would only make the immediate situation more difficult. But she did ask him, one night, if he had never considered divorcing her for desertion in these ten years.

'You could have, couldn't you, Adam?' Christine asked, conscious of Valerie suddenly very still, at the other side of the fire. 'Or — or you could have got a divorce presuming I was dead, perhaps?'

'I could have,' Adam agreed after a moment, carefully. And then he smiled, and touched her hand gently. 'But I didn't, did I?'

He talks to me as if I was a child, Christine thought suddenly, coldly. And not a particularly bright child at that.

'You should be very glad Adam didn't divorce you, Christine,' Valerie put in, unexpectedly.

Christine looked at her, surprised, realizing that now the whole thing was becoming too much for Valerie, the situation in this house was making her tense and on edge.

With shame, she knew that she had very little sympathy for Valerie, and this bothered her, to be so lacking in generosity. She determined to try harder to meet Valerie's efforts at friendliness half way, and she determined to try harder to see Valerie's point of view. Here she was, after years of waiting patiently for Adam, perhaps just reaching the point where he might have considered getting a divorce for desertion, and then, out of the blue, his wife turns up. And in circumstances that made it almost impossible to discuss divorce or separation for quite a while.

No, Christine told herself, all things considered, no wonder Valerie feels it isn't easy to be glad I came back. And she tries so hard, she really does. I must try much harder.

And so, when Valerie took to bringing her a mug of warm milk when she went to bed, Christine accepted it, although she never had been fond of warm milk. Valerie would sit on the bed while she drank it, and talk. And Christine, tired and on edge herself, could do nothing but wish she would go, with her constant reminders to take her pills, and her solicitousness. But she told herself, over and over again, that Valerie meant well, that all her efforts deserved a warmer reception.

'Yes, I've taken my pill,' she replied to Valerie one night, latish. 'Listen — wasn't that Jenny coming in?'

'Don't get out of bed, Christine, you'll catch cold,' Valerie told her. 'Stay here and drink your milk.'

'I want to say goodnight to Jenny,' Christine replied, all at once determined. She pulled her dressing-gown and slippers on, and hurried across to Jenny's room.

'Jenny?'

Jenny opened the door, and there was now no instant defensiveness in her eyes.

'What are you doing out of bed, Mummy?' she said, smiling. 'Dad said you'd been up for ages, that's why I didn't look in.' Suddenly, unexpectedly, a little awkwardly, she kissed Christine's cheek. 'Go back to bed — I'll come in and tell you all about the hop before I go in the morning.'

Christine went back to her own room, an ache of happiness in her throat, thinking only of Jenny, of the brightness of her young face, the — the affection there had been in her eyes, so that it was almost a shock to open the door of her room and find Valerie still there with her warm milk.

'I don't want any milk, thanks, Valerie,' Christine told her, with a flash of rebellion. 'I'm sure I'll sleep without it.'

'Drink it now that it's here,' Valerie urged. She smiled. 'I sleep so well myself that I don't like to think of you not sleeping.'

Resigned, Christine drank the milk quickly. And as Valerie left her, a startling thought came to her. The warm milk, and the insistence on Christine obeying the doctor and taking a sleeping pill — tied up with the memory of Adam's voice, lazy at first, and then suddenly rough as he talked to Valerie —

Warm colour flooded Christine's cheeks at the thought that perhaps Valerie wanted to make quite certain that she slept well, for her own very good reasons. I must talk to Adam soon, she thought, sleepily, I must tell him that I want him to have his freedom.

She slept, then, sooner than she had

expected to. Then there were wild dreams, wild and frightening, when she was struggling to wake from some nightmare and knowing that she wasn't going to be able to. Dreams when she was running round the corner towards the old cottage, only to find there was nothing but a blackened ruin there. Dreams when Dr Ruthven was there, and he was telling her to do something, and shouting at her because she wouldn't or couldn't understand.

And then, at last, she was struggling into wakefulness and Dr Ruthven was there. Adam was there too, and Valerie. And Jenny, white and frightened, close to tears.

Christine could feel her forehead damp and clammy with sweat, and her head ached terribly, with a dull and leaden ache.

'What's wrong?' she whispered, afraid, looking up at the doctor.

'Nothing now, Mrs Lawrence,' he told her, gravely. 'But you gave us quite a fright — especially when this young lady came in and found you.'

'What do you mean?' Christine asked, bewildered. 'Have I been ill?'

'In a way, yes,' the doctor agreed, and his blue eyes were concerned. 'When I gave you these sleeping-pills, Mrs Lawrence, I made it quite clear that you were to take only one each night.'

'But I did take only one,' Christine told him. 'I don't always take one, but you said I should, you said — '

Under his direct gaze, her voice faltered.

'I only took one,' she told him again, shakily.

'You took six, Mrs Lawrence,' the doctor said quietly. The wrappings are there in your waste-paper basket.'

'Six!' Christine repeated, shocked. 'But I couldn't have, you told me it was dangerous to take more than — more than — '

And now, looking from face to face, she could see all too clearly what they were thinking. Either she had deliberately taken an overdose, or — she had done it without knowing, which was possibly even worse.

'I didn't take more than one,' she said again, managing to speak steadily now. 'Valerie — you were here, you saw me take one.'

Valerie looked at her, and then looked away.

'I did see you take only one, Christine,' she agreed. 'But — there were six papers in the basket.'

Adam hadn't said anything, and Christine turned to him, desperately.

'Adam — you know I wouldn't take more, knowing they were dangerous,' she said, shakily.

He hesitated.

'I know you wouldn't mean to,' he agreed after a moment. 'But — perhaps you took them without knowing it, Christine.'

She shook her head, stubbornly, unable to say anything more. And then she saw Jenny's face, her wide frightened eyes, and she stretched out her hand.

'Don't look like that, Jenny darling,' she said unsteadily.

The girl's hand gripped hers hard.

'I'm all right, I promise you,' she said. Then she turned to the doctor. 'I don't know how this has happened, but — I'm certain I didn't take six tablets. Can't we just — forget about this?'

The doctor hesitated, and behind her, she was conscious of Adam giving a fractional shake of his head.

'I don't know, Mrs Lawrence,' Dr Ruthven said, slowly. 'I'd like to believe you, but — the fact is that you had six tablets, you were in a coma, your daughter couldn't rouse you. Now — you must see that we can't have this sort of thing happening.'

There was something she had to know.

'Six tablets,' she asked him. 'Would that much have — have killed me?'

'No,' he replied, definitely. 'Even without using the stomach-pump, six wouldn't have killed you.' He turned to Adam. 'Can I have a word with you, Mr Lawrence?'

They went out of the room, and Jenny, with a convulsive shudder, went out too. For a moment Valerie and Christine looked at each other, both equally uncomfortable, and then Valerie murmured something about a cup of tea, and went out too.

All at once Christine realized how tired she was — tired and sore, presumably from the stomach-pump. She lay back on her pillows and closed her eyes.

'Mrs Lawrence,' Dr Ruthven said. Christine opened her eyes and looked at him. 'Mrs Lawrence, I'm sorry, but I'm going to insist on you coming in for further observation. There are a couple of other fellows I'd like you to see as well, and I've just rung them. This is Tuesday — we'd like you to come in on Friday.'

She could see that there was to be no arguing with him, and so she said nothing.

'And in the meanwhile,' he said, kindly, 'take things easy — don't over-tire yourself. Goodbye — see you on Friday.'

A few minutes after the front door closed behind him, Adam, a little awkward and constrained, came back up to say that the doctor thought she should have a sleep now for a bit.

'I've had too much sleep,' Christine replied, knowing she sounded sulky, but knowing too that he could have prevented this examination in the hospital, if he had tried. If he had wanted to.

'Adam,' she said slowly, 'what is likely to happen after this — this examination?'

He stood at the door, obviously anxious to be gone.

'I don't know,' he said at last, with reluctance.

But his eyes avoided hers.

'I think you do know,' Christine said, surprising herself by her firmness.

'He said something about perhaps some treatment in a special nursing-home,' Adam replied after a while.

'Christine — I really have to go, it's almost eleven now, and I have people to see.'

When he had gone, she lay back again, her forehead clammy once more. A special nursing-home? Mental treatment, obviously.

Which I don't need, Christine told herself sharply. And — if it hadn't been for these tablets —

She closed her eyes and tried to think clearly, past the woolliness in her head. Because she had taken six tablets instead of one, Dr Ruthven was convinced there was still something wrong with her, convinced that she needed special treatment.

But I didn't take six tablets, Christine told herself, and now, suddenly, the drowsiness and groping in her head cleared. She knew that she hadn't taken six tablets, she knew she had taken only one. But the fact remained that she had had six tablets. And — if she hadn't taken them herself, then someone else must have given them to her.

It was so obvious that Christine could only blame the muzziness of the sleeping pills for her failure to see the truth before. There was only one person who could have given her six tablets — dissolved in the milk last night.

But why should Valerie do that? To make quite certain that Christine was asleep and not — interfering, in any way? Why six? Wouldn't one or even two have done?

Maybe she didn't realize, Christine thought, trying to find an explanation. Maybe she thought they were milder than they are.

At first she thought that she would tax Valerie with this, or perhaps tell Adam. Then that didn't seem such a good idea, and a better one came to Christine. She would wait, and on Friday she would go to hospital as arranged, and she would tell Dr Ruthven the whole story — about Adam and Valerie being in love, about her certainty that Valerie had given her the sleeping-pills. Until then, she would say nothing.

In the meantime, she would do nothing and say nothing. She wouldn't take her sleeping pills, even if she didn't sleep at all, and she wouldn't take any warm milk from Valerie. Not even to keep her from suspecting.

It wasn't easy, the next day, to behave normally and naturally with Valerie and with Adam. But Christine was determined that nothing else was going to happen that could be passed on to Dr Ruthven as further 'proof' of her lack of mental balance. She refused, pleasantly but firmly, the warm milk that Valerie brought her, and she refused equally firmly Valerie's offer to take her across to the boutique with her.

'You must be lonely here, Christine,' Valerie said, concerned.

'I'm quite happy,' Christine replied. 'I'll take the dogs out, and I'll do some more knitting — I'm rather enjoying being lazy, Valerie.'

She picked up her knitting, knowing

that Valerie was looking at her doubtfully, knowing that she was disturbed. All I have to do, she told herself, is to get through the days until Friday. Then I'll tell Dr Ruthven, and — everything should be all right.

When she went down for breakfast on Thursday morning, she knew that she had walked in on a scene. Adam and Valerie were standing together, and Jenny facing them, flushed and truculent. It was too late to back out, so Christine stood there, awkward, embarrassed.

'Go to your room, Jenny,' Adam said after a moment. 'I'll talk to you later.'

Unwilling to interfere, Christine couldn't resist giving Jenny a swift glance of sympathy as the girl walked out, head high.

'Trouble with Jenny?' she asked, as the door closed.

Adam and Valerie glanced at each other, quickly, and Christine, watching them, was certain that they were wondering just how much she had heard before she came in.

'Yes, a little,' Valerie replied after a moment. She smiled. 'She's got this stupid idea that there's no need for you to go to hospital tomorrow — she even said she was going to ring Dr Ruthven and tell him that you were perfectly all right, that you didn't need any further examination or treatment, all you needed was to be left alone.'

Good for Jenny, Christine thought, delighted, sitting down at the table. But she said nothing, and after a moment Valerie began to ask Adam, brightly, about his morning, then to tell them both about the fashion show she was arranging in one of the big city shops.

Christine hoped to have a word with Jenny before she went, but Adam called to Jenny to hurry, and there was no chance. I'll talk to her this afternoon, Christine promised herself. I'll try to make her see that she needn't worry about me seeing Dr Ruthven, that it's the best way to get things sorted out.

But it was one of the days when

Jenny had a class in the late afternoon, and she came in just in time to join them at the table, slipping in quickly, breathlessly, avoiding her father's eyes, and smiling a little uncertainly at Christine.

'What did you do today?' she asked her mother.

'Some more of my knitting,' Christine told her, and Jenny smiled, for although nothing had been said, she knew that the ribbed sweater was for her. 'And then I took the dogs out — we had a lovely walk.'

Across the table, Valerie looked at her, sharply.

'Did you shut them in the back, Christine?' she asked.

'Of course I did,' Christine replied, forcing herself to keep her voice even. 'I always do.'

'Are you certain?' Valerie persisted, and Christine, in spite of herself, couldn't help flushing with annoyance.

Then Valerie turned to Adam.

'I just realized,' she said, her voice

worried, 'that when I went through to the kitchen just now I didn't hear them scratching at the door, and you know they always do when they're shut in the back. Jenny — go and have a look, dear, just to set my mind at rest.'

Jenny, obviously alarmed excused herself and hurried through to the kitchen. They heard her open the door, and they heard her call and whistle. Then she came back, white-faced.

'They're not there,' she said. She turned to Christine. 'Are you certain you closed the back gate?' she asked, and the accusation in her voice made all the colour drain from Christine's face.

'Of course I am, Jenny,' she said, as steadily as she could. 'I always do when I've taken them out.'

Jenny turned to her father.

'I'm going out to look for them,' she told him. And without another word to Christine, she went out of the room.

'What can we do, Adam?' Valerie murmured. 'You know how Jenny is about these dogs.'

Adam stood up.

'I'll phone the police,' he said, quietly. 'You know how they are on the roads — no sense at all.'

I did close the gate, Christine told herself, with certainty. Half an hour later, when Jenny came in, she said that to her.

'It's open now, anyway,' Jenny said shakily, not bothering to be polite. 'And my dogs are gone.'

An hour later, there was a phone call from the Animal Welfare people, whom Adam had also contacted. Christine, beside him, saw his mouth tighten as he listened.

'I see,' he said quietly. 'No — I understand. Thank you very much for all you've done. I'll be over right away to collect him.'

He put down the 'phone and called to Jenny, who was out at the back again looking for the dogs. When she came in, she stopped, seeing her father's face.

'They've found them?' she asked unsteadily.

He shook his head.

'I'm sorry, Jenny — they've found Guy, but — Doll has been run over. I'll go now and bring him home. Do you want to come with me?'

It was a long time before Jenny managed to speak.

'I'll come,' she whispered. 'They've always been together, since they were pups, he'll miss her so much.'

Christine went across the room to her.

'Jenny darling, I'm so sorry this has happened.'

'Sorry?' Jenny laughed, a high, unnatural laugh. 'So you should be — if it hadn't been for you it wouldn't have happened.'

'Jenny, I promise you I did close that gate,' Christine said, steadily.

'You can promise whatever you like, but — but my dog is still dead.' Jenny turned abruptly and went out of the room, and now tears were streaming down her cheeks.

'No, Christine,' Adam said, sharply,

as Christine made to follow the girl. 'Leave her alone. These dogs meant a great deal to Jenny — this is going to take some time for her to get over. If I were you I'd say as little as possible for a bit.'

He went out then, and in a moment Christine heard him call for Jenny, heard them both go out and into the car. She sat down, realizing now how shaken she was by what had happened.

Then Valerie came in, with a cup of tea for her.

'Adam told me what has happened,' she said. 'Christine — I think you should have a cup of tea and go to bed — it might be better if you weren't around when Jenny comes back.'

Christine lifted her head and looked at the other woman.

'I did close that gate, Valerie,' she said unhappily.

'I'm sure you did,' Valerie returned quickly — too quickly. 'But unfortunately Jenny is quite certain that you didn't.'

Christine looked at her. Her thoughts whirled. Jenny had been the only one who said that there was nothing wrong with Christine. But — now Jenny too felt that Christine wasn't responsible for her actions.

'You opened that gate, Valerie,' Christine said, her voice low.

And in the moment before the other woman answered, Christine saw something in her dark eyes that told her that she was right. And told her much more, too.

'Christine, dear, why should I do that?' Valerie returned, lightly. 'You're over-tired, you should go to bed — remember you're going to hospital tomorrow.'

'Yes, I am,' Christine agreed, managing to control her voice. 'And when I go, Valerie, I'm going to tell Dr Ruthven everything.'

'Everything?' Valerie asked, sharply. 'What do you mean?'

All at once Christine wished she had said nothing. But it was too late now, she had to go on.

'I'm going to tell him about the list, and about the sleeping pills,' she said, and she could feel her heart thudding unevenly.

'I wouldn't, if I were you,' Valerie returned, softly.

Startled, Christine looked at her.

'Because Adam and I have already talked to him,' Valerie went on, and the cold hostility in her dark eyes shook Christine. 'We've warned him that you seem to have these — delusions, that people are persecuting you, that people are trying to harm you.' She lit a cigarette and leaned back in her chair. 'So he'll be very interested when you confirm this yourself. I should think he'll be very sympathetic, and he'll probably suggest that a good long rest — well away from all these unpleasant people who are doing such nasty things — is the best thing for you.'

Adam and I.

Somehow, that shook Christine more than anything else Valerie had said.

Until now, she had thought that this petty persecution came only from Valerie. But Adam too?

Blindly, Christine stood up.

'I'm going to bed,' she said, suddenly unable even to be in the same room as Valerie.

There was a tightness in her chest, and she felt as if she couldn't get enough air. In her room, she sat down on the bed, and buried her face in her hands. She was beyond tears, beyond coherent thought. She didn't know how long she sat there, with waves of panic sweeping over her, before she could begin to think clearly again.

The first thing she did, then, was to rise and lock her door.

When she had done that, she sat down again on the bed. And she knew that she wasn't going to the hospital tomorrow, she wasn't going to see Dr Ruthven and tell him anything. Because it wouldn't be any use.

I've got to get away from here, she thought then, knowing it was the only thing she could do. For a moment, there was the tearing pain of leaving Jenny, but when she remembered the way Jenny had looked at her tonight, she knew that this time Valerie had done her work well, this had undone all the precarious regrowth of any relationship between Jenny and her. I won't give Jenny up, Christine thought with certainty. But — first I've got to get away, I've got to think about all this.

And as she thought that, she knew where she would go to.

It was a slender chance — such a slim fragment of a hope that at the time she had thought nothing more about it, had dismissed it from her mind. But it was the only slight clue she had.

Tormore.

The village in the Western Highlands that John Scott, the man at the party, had mentioned, the village where he had thought he had once seen her.

There had been nothing in the name that woke any echoes in Christine's memory, and there was still nothing.

And when she thought back to the conversation she had had with him, she knew that she was building on very little. He had said that he must have been wrong, that the woman he had seen was not as like her as he had thought at first. And he had said, too, that it had been years ago.

But it was all she had to build on, and Christine knew that she would go there.

She lay on her bed until the household was quiet, until long after she heard Adam and Jenny come back. Desperately she longed to go to Jenny, to comfort her for the loss of her dog, to take the girl in her arms. But she knew how any attempt at friendship would be received by Jenny tonight, and so she remained in her room.

Very late, she heard Adam and Valerie talking, and she heard someone try the handle of her door, softly, and heard Adam call her name. She lay still, hardly even breathing, and at last they went away.

Then Christine rose, and packed a small bag. She had no suitcase, only a zip shopping bag. She put a few things in, and all the money she had — Adam had been generous, giving her money without asking what she intended spending it on — and now, coldly and dispassionately, she was glad of this. Then she dressed in warm slacks and a thick jersey, and her short sheepskin-lined coat. There was no point in going now, in the middle of the night, but she knew that she must be ready to go at the first light, before anyone stirred.

She didn't sleep at all, and very early the next morning she unlocked her door and quietly crept downstairs. There was a moment of sheer panic, when she heard a movement from the housekeeper's room, beside the kitchen, and she froze. But nothing happened, and she unlocked the front door and went outside.

It was bitterly cold, and she was glad of the thick coat, glad of her warm boots and gloves. She had to walk two streets before reaching a bus route, and she walked briskly, glad to be able to warm up. It was still early when she reached Prince's Street — too early to go and see John Scott. She went into a cafe and had a cup of coffee, clasping her hands around the big cup, and a toasted roll.

Now, in the grey morning light, she began to have doubts about what she was doing. A chance resemblance that even this man had later disclaimed — it was nothing to go on, really. And yet — it was all she had.

She realized that the waitress was looking at her curiously, for she had been there far longer than most people, who rushed in, drank a cup of coffee, and then hurried out again. She rose, paid for her coffee, and went out, into the early morning rush of Prince's Street.

It was a misty morning, and the Castle loomed out of the mist above her. And once again, there was the faint, hardly discernible stirring in her memory, some groping feeling that once before she had stood looking at the Castle, and knowing that she was leaving it, leaving the old city she loved. A memory of dreadful sorrow.

'You all right?' a woman said curiously, bumping into Christine as she stood there.

'Yes — yes, thank you, I'm all right,' Christine replied, shaken back into herself.

Determinedly, she turned towards the Star offices. When she asked the girl at the desk if she could see Mr John Scott, the girl asked her if she had an appointment.

'No, I haven't,' Christine replied.

'I'm sorry, but Mr Scott is very busy,' the girl told her, politely, regretfully.

Christine hesitated. Then, determined she wasn't giving up so easily, she asked for paper and a pencil, and she scribbled a note.

'Mr Scott, I must see you urgently. It's about Tormore. Christine Lawrence.'

She folded it, and asked the girl if it

could be taken to Mr Scott. Then she waited, more than half expecting a message to be brought back to say that Mr Scott was still too busy to see her.

But after a few minutes the phone at the desk rang, and the girl answered it.

'Mr Scott will see you,' she said. 'Come through this way, please.'

John Scott rose from his desk and came to lead Christine to a chair at the other side of his huge desk.

'You look as if you could do with a cup of strong tea,' he said, looking at her sharply. He rang a bell, and a few moments later a tray of tea was brought in. John Scott poured two big cups, and without consulting her, stirred in plenty sugar.

'Drink that and then tell me what's wrong, lass,' he said, and the unexpected kindness in his voice brought a blur of tears to Christine's eyes.

'Right,' he said when she had finished, taking the cup from her. 'What is it?'

'I want to go to Tormore,' Christine told him.

The shaggy white eyebrows rose, but he said nothing.

'I — have to get away from here,' she went on, painfully. 'And if there's any chance at all that anyone in this place knows me, I must try to find out.' She looked across the desk at the elderly man. 'Mr Scott — please don't tell — my husband that I came here. I — don't want him to know where I've gone.'

'He'll be upset, and worried, lass,' John Scott pointed out.

Christine shook her head numbly, remembering that by now she should have been in the hospital, with Dr Ruthven more than inclined to find that she was — neurotic, unbalanced. No, Adam wouldn't be worried. He would talk to Valerie, and they would know why she had gone.

'You can't tell me any more?' the man at the other side of the desk asked, gently.

'No, I — I'm sorry, I can't,' Christine replied. 'But — he won't worry, Mr Scott, he'll know why I've gone.'

He was still hesitant.

'You mustn't build anything on Tormore, Mrs Lawrence,' he said after a moment. 'It was a long time ago, and as I said, I'm certain I was mistaken. And besides — '

He stopped, and Christine waited.

'Besides,' he went on, after a moment, 'I don't think you could have been there. Adam seems certain that you've spent most of these ten years in a — hospital, somewhere.'

'In a hospital?' Christine repeated, bewildered. 'But why should I have been in a hospital?'

'In a mental hospital,' the older man told her, gently.

She couldn't grasp this.

'But no one knows where I've been,' she said, confused. 'I — it seems I went away ten years ago, and then — then just came back, out of the blue. That's why I want to get to Tormore, in case that is where I've been, in case someone there — remembers me.' She shook her head. 'I can't understand why Adam should think I've been in a — in a mental hospital. He's never said anything to me about that.'

'He didn't say much,' John Scott said, watching her. 'It was perhaps more an impression he gave some of us.'

With horror, Christine began to understand. A slight impression that perhaps that was where she had been, added to the suggestion that she might have to go back into some mental hospital — she could see more clearly now what had been happening.

'I don't know why he didn't just divorce me, either for desertion or — or presuming that I was dead,' she whispered, not caring now that this man was a stranger. 'He must have wanted that.'

John Scott filled up both their cups and passed hers back to her.

'You know Adam has ambitions for Parliament?' he said, after a moment.

Christine looked at him, not under-standing.

'We're funny folks in Edinburgh,' he said, almost apologetically. 'Rather old-fashioned — we don't look too kindly on divorce, unless for a very good reason. Could be some folks whose vote Adam might want would look a little askance on a divorce.' He shrugged. 'I don't know, but that's how Adam might look on it.' He stirred his tea. 'I knew your folks,' he said abruptly. 'You were Christine Morrison, weren't you? Knew your father well. Terrible business, that train crash, both of them together. You hadn't been married long then, had you?'

'Not very long,' Christine said, remembering the bleak horror of that time, remembering that it had only been the tiny Jenny who had helped her then. 'Mr Scott, I want to ask you a favour. Will you — will you keep an eye on Jenny for me? Without letting — Adam — know where I am? Could you do that?'

'I'll do that.' He hesitated. 'You have to take the Inverness train, and once you're there you change, and then at Fort William you take a bus. Will you manage that, lass? Have you any money?'

'I'll manage,' Christine told him steadily. With an effort, she smiled. 'I have enough money, I think. Thank you for everything, Mr Scott.'

He looked at his watch.

'I wish I could take you to the station, but I have a conference.'

He came to the door with her.

'If you run into any difficulties, will you get in touch with me?' he asked, abruptly. 'I don't like to feel you're so much on your own.'

Once again Christine's eyes blurred with tears.

'I'll do that, Mr Scott,' she promised, shakily. 'And — thank you.'

Surprising herself, then, she kissed his cheek and then hurried out.

She hadn't long to wait for a train, and although she told herself there was no way Adam could know where she was, no chance of him or Valerie following her, she was glad when she was in the train, when it was speeding out of Edinburgh.

As far as she knew, she had never been in Inverness in her life, but when she came out of the station, blinking a little in the surprising winter sunshine, she knew that there was a tearoom across the road. She told herself that this was only logical, to think that a tearoom would be near the station. And yet, as she sat waiting for tea and sandwiches, she had the growing certainty that she had been here before, a complete familiarity with the room, even with the willow pattern china.

In Fort William, too, there was the sense of recognition. She walked up past the museum, and she thought of the drinking cup that had belonged to Prince Charlie, wondering, a little afraid, how she had known that. Then, from the steamers in the harbour, she heard sirens sounding, and there was a swift, dizzying memory of hurrying down the narrow streets to meet — to meet someone, she didn't know who. But — someone she was so glad to be meeting. For although she couldn't remember anything else, she could remember the swift flooding joy as she heard the siren and hurried down to the harbour.

And she began, then, to feel that she had been right to come here, that whatever instinct had helped her to make the decision had been right. For she knew where the bus to Tormore would be waiting.

It was almost dark, and she could see nothing as the bus wound its way through the narrow country roads. Then through a pass, with mountains high on either side, and through into the glen beyond. And she knew as the bus drew up in the centre of the village, that she was in Tormore.

Back in Tormore.

It was dark and it was cold, and Christine told herself that the only sensible thing to do was to stay the night at the hotel here in the village, and see what she was going to do the next day.

But even while admitting that it was the sensible thing to do, she knew that she wasn't going to do it.

She came out of the bus and stood in the village square, beside the war memorial, undecided, and sick disappointment swept over her. Somehow, she had expected that when she got out of the bus here she would know. She would recognize the village, and she would know where she wanted to go. True, there had been a moment when she saw the War Memorial, a moment of familiarity, but — nothing more.

'Are you wanting to go to the Big House, miss?' a child beside her asked, shyly.

The Big House?

'Which way is it?' Christine asked, forcing herself to keep her voice steady.

'Across the wee bridge, and up the

drive beyond it,' the child told her, pointing.

Christine lifted her bag and went along out of the light of the village. Just beyond the little stone bridge, with the plaque on it that said it was built by General Wade — and how did I know that, Christine wondered, her heart thudding with excitement, when I can't see it in the dark? — there was a light at the start of the drive. The Big House, she thought, and she wondered if she did want to go there. But now it seemed easier to go on than to turn back, and she went on up the dark, tree-lined drive.

Once, an owl hooted, driving all the breath from her body with sudden fright. But why should I be afraid of an owl, she thought, when I'm so used to hearing them?

The thought, and its certainty, made her stand still for a moment. Then she went on, knowing all at once that beyond the next corner there would be the lights of the Big House.

There it stood, squat and solid, as she

had known it would. And yet — there was still no actual chord of memory touched, there was nothing more tangible than feelings, than vague pockets of recognition.

Slowly, she went across to the door and lifted the knocker, knowing as she did so the sound it would make, reverberating through the big old house.

When the door opened a boy stood there, a boy who looked at her for a moment, and then grinned, his freckled nose and his red hair suddenly, achingly familiar.

But yet she didn't know him, didn't know who he was.

'She's here,' he called. 'Doctor Neil, she's here!'

Then there was a man there, a man striding down the corridor towards her. He was tall — tall and lean, his dark hair untidy, his eyes dark in the brown of his face.

'Chris!' he said, and he took both her hands in his. 'Chris, you've come back!'

5

He looked down at her, and his hands were still hard on hers.

'Why were you so long, Chris?' he asked, and the tender roughness of his voice made her heart turn over.

'I'm sorry,' she whispered, not knowing how to tell him that she didn't remember him, that she didn't understand what he meant.

He lifted her bag, and turned to the boy.

'Go and tell Maggie to put a bottle in Chris's bed, Keith,' he said.

It was only then, when the boy went off down the corridor ahead of them, that Christine saw that one leg was in calipers.

'Come in and tell me everything,' the tall dark man said, taking her into a small untidy room, with a fire burning brightly in the hearth. 'Sit down and get warm — you're frozen, love.'

He rubbed her hands, warming them. And all at once it was too much for Christine — the welcome on the boy's face, the way this man had said her name, the easy tenderness of his voice when he called her love — and the warmth in her hands and through her whole body because she had found him. Found him — and yet she didn't even know his name.

'Don't cry, love,' he said, not quite steadily, and he took out a handkerchief and wiped her eyes. 'It's all over — how did it go?'

Her tears had stopped. Christine drew a deep, shuddering breath.

'Will you tell me your name, please?' she asked him.

All the colour left his face as he looked down at her.

'What's wrong, Chris?' he asked, and she could see that he was controlling himself, forcing himself to keep his voice level.

'I — seem to have had a sort of

black-out,' Christine told him, not looking at him. 'I'm sorry, but I don't remember who you are.'

His hands gripped her arms, hard.

'Is this some sort of joke?' he asked, his voice low. 'Are you trying to tell me you're going back to him?'

'I'm trying to tell you the truth,' Christine returned, shakily. 'Please — who are you?'

His hands dropped from her arms, and unconsciously she rubbed the bruised flesh.

'I'm Neil Ferguson,' he told her. 'Chris — for heavens's sake what has happened to you?'

'I don't know,' Christine told him unhappily. 'I — I found myself in Edinburgh, with ten years missing from my life.'

He was quiet, waiting. Christine looked away from him, into the fire.

'I didn't know I'd lost ten years,' she said. 'I was — I was looking for my little girl, in the park, and I couldn't find her.' For a moment, she closed her eyes, the growing terror coming back to her, the gradual realization that Jenny had gone, that she wasn't there. 'Then I thought she might have gone to her father's office, and I was going to go there, but I was knocked down by a car. I — I've been in hospital for quite a while.' She wanted to say his name, but something held her back.

'Go on, Chris,' Neil Ferguson said quietly.

She looked at him now, at the gleam of firelight on the dark leanness of his face, on the dark hair.

'I couldn't tell them for quite a while who I was or where I lived, but then I did, and my — my husband came. I was still worried about Jenny, but he said she was all right, he said she was at home. But they wouldn't let me see her, they wouldn't even let me talk to her on the phone. And — then they told me what had happened.'

Unconsciously, she stretched out her hand and he took it.

'They told me that ten years ago I

walked out, I left Adam and Jenny. They told me that Jenny was seventeen, not seven.'

'I don't understand,' Neil Ferguson said, bewildered. 'Did you see Jenny?'

'Yes, I — I saw her when Adam took me back to the house.' She shrugged. 'The doctor said there is no real explanation for this sort of thing, that it just happens.'

'He's right, but there's usually a pretty good reason for this blanking out a period of your life,' Neil Ferguson replied, absently. He ran his hands through his dark hair, started to say something and, then, glancing at her, seemed to change his mind.

'Why did you come back here?' he asked. 'Did you remember something?'

Christine shook her head.

'No, I didn't remember anything,' she told him. Then she told him about meeting John Scott, about his mention of this resemblance to someone he had seen in Tormore.

'Does your husband know you've

come back here?' Neil Ferguson asked then.

Christine shook her head.

'I just came away,' she said, her voice low, unable to hide her distress. 'I had to get away, and I asked Mr Scott where Tormore was.'

'Why did you have to get away, Chris?' he asked, gently.

But she shook her head, unable to say any more.

He stood up, and his hand on her shoulder was gentle.

'Sit there at the fire, love,' he told her. 'I'm going to get Maggie to bring us a cup of tea. Have you had anything to eat today?'

She couldn't remember at first, then she thought of the little tearoom in Inverness, and told him.

He went out then, and she waited at the fire, realizing now just how tired she was, how drained of everything. When he came back, he had a big tray with tea and sandwiches on it.

'I told Maggie to go to bed,' he said,

'she's so keen to see you, but I said she can wait until morning. And the boys can wait too.'

'The boys?' she asked, not understanding.

'You know about the boys,' he told her quietly, reassuringly. 'You'll remember, in time. They're all boys who have been in trouble of some kind, you could say they're on probation. But they also need medical care, that's why I've got them here.' He hesitated, and then in the same oddly gentle voice, he said, 'That's why you are here, Chris. You help to look after them.'

He took her cup from her.

'Had enough?' he asked.

Christine nodded.

'Right, you're going to bed — you're exhausted,' he told her briskly.

Christine stood up, unwillingly.

'But there's so much I have to ask you, so much I must know,' she said.

He touched her cheek, gently.

'Time for that tomorrow, love,' he told her. 'Come along, Maggie's put a bottle in your bed — she's aired it regularly, we — kept hoping you would be back any time.'

He took her upstairs, and opened a door at the end of a long corridor. It was a small room, small and homely — very different from the room that had been hers in the house in Edinburgh. There was a fireplace, with a fire burning in it, and the bedcover was a patchwork quilt. Christine looked around her wondering how long this room had been hers.

'Goodnight, Chris, I'll see you in the morning,' Neil Ferguson said.

'Wait, Neil.'

Warm colour flooded her cheeks at the easy way his name had come to her lips.

'Wait,' she said again. 'There are two things I must ask you.'

'Don't rush things, Chris,' he advised. 'Take it easy.'

She shook her head.

'But you've got to tell me this, I must know.' In spite of herself, her voice shook, and she was close to tears. 'Did I know you ten years ago? Did I leave Adam because of you?'

'Chris, love.'

With two strides, he was across the room, and he had taken her in his arms, holding her close to him, without passion, wanting, she knew, only to comfort her.

'Is that what you've been thinking?'

'I didn't know,' Christine whispered.

He tilted her chin so that she had to look up at him.

'For the moment,' he said steadily, 'all you need to know is this. You left your husband because you were bitterly unhappy. You came to Inverness, and I met you there, I offered you a job helping here. But — Chris, you didn't leave him because of me, I promise you that — you only met me after you'd left him.'

The other thing, too had to be asked now, so that she knew where she stood.

'When I went away from here,' she said, her voice low, 'why did I go?'

His hands dropped, and he looked down at her, unsmiling.

'You went away,' he told her, 'to ask your husband for a divorce, so that you could marry me.'

He went to the door, but then he hesitated, and came back to her.

'Goodnight, Chris,' he said, gently. His lips touched hers briefly, warmly. 'Goodnight, my love.'

Then he was gone. But her lips were still warm from the touch of his, and she remembered how right had been the feeling of his arms around her.

Slowly, she got ready for bed. And in spite of everything, she couldn't help smiling a little when she drew the bedcovers down and saw the old-fashioned stone hotwater bottle, with warm flannelette pyjamas wound round it.

She got into bed and put her feet on the hot stone bottle, and all at once it was right and familiar to her — far more familiar than the electric blanket in her room in Edinburgh had been.

Much to her own surprise, Christine fell asleep quickly, and soundly, waking to find her room quite light. The fire was still burning brightly, and she thought that someone — Maggie, perhaps? — had come in and built it up.

I should get up, she thought sleepily, stretching in the bed, still warm under the patchwork quilt. It was a long time, she realized, since she'd had as good a night's sleep.

'Are you awake, Chris?' a voice asked peremptorily from the door.

Maggie, Chris thought it must be.

'Yes — come in,' she called.

The door opened, and a tiny white-haired woman came in. Her dark eyes were bright and warm, and they rested on Chris, quickly, shrewdly, as she put the tray down beside the bed.

'Breakfast in bed today, tomorrow you get up like you've always done,' she said in a business-like voice. 'I'm Maggie — Neil says you've lost your memory. My, but you're thin, lassie

— we'll need to build you up. Now eat every bite of that porridge and the bacon and eggs — the boys helped to make it for you, they're that pleased you're home. Just give a shout if you want any more tea.'

She handed Christine the tray, and went out, leaving Christine a little breathless, but relieved at the casual, easy mention of her lost memory, glad not to have to make any more explanations.

To her own surprise, she was hungry, and she did as Maggie had ordered, and finished everything. Then she got up, and washed at the little wash-hand basin in her room. Hesitantly, she opened the cupboard, all at once unwilling to wear the clothes she had come in yesterday.

She took out a pair of denim jeans, obviously old and well worn, and put them on, with a thick brown jersey that was in the cupboard too. The trousers were too loose at the waist, and she realized that she must have lost quite a bit of weight. She pulled on the thick jersey, and brushed her hair back from her face. There was some makeup in the cupboard, and she put a soft pink lipstick on.

Then she made her bed and went downstairs, carrying the tray and the stone hot-water bottle. It was cold in the corridors, and she was glad of the thick jersey and the warm socks and stout shoes she had found. At the bottom of the stairs she hesitated, then, hearing Maggie's voice raised in 'Rock of Ages', she followed the sound of it to the kitchen.

Keith, the red-haired boy, and another boy with a dark, withdrawn face, were doing the washing-up.

'Hi, Chris,' Keith said cheerfully. 'Doctor Neil says you don't remember who we are or anything, so I'd better tell you. I'm Keith — you know me, but Ted here is new.'

'Hello, Keith — Ted,' Chris replied, a little awkwardly, but again glad that there was no need for further explanations.

'Just give the boys your dishes, Chris,' Maggie told her. 'And you can come and give me a hand with peeling the tatties for dinner.'

They had almost finished the huge pot of potatoes when Neil Ferguson came in.

'Finished my rounds early today,' he said cheerfully. 'You look better already, Chris. Sleep well?'

'Very well, thanks,' Chris replied, furious with herself for the warm colour that flooded her cheeks now that she knew the relationship between herself and this man. She turned back to peeling the potatoes.

'Any tea?' Neil asked.

'You're too early,' Maggie told him firmly. 'We're just finished clearing up breakfast. If you're through your rounds, why not take Chris for a bit of a walk, and then come back and you might find some tea made?'

She took the knife from Christine's hand, and said that she would finish them herself.

'Get your coat,' she advised. 'It's a raw morning, real December weather.'

Christine ran upstairs and lifted her warm coat from the chair where she had put it the night before. She looked in the cupboard, but there was nothing as warm as this, and it seemed foolish not to wear it.

Neil was waiting for her at the foot of the stairs, and he wore a thick brown sweater much like her own, under his duffle coat.

'You look more like yourself,' he said, and she flushed at the approval in his eyes.

'Did I knit that jersey for you?' she asked, not meaning to, but unable to stop herself.

He looked down at her, and smiled.

'Yes, you did,' he told her. 'You made a much better job of it, too, than you did of the first one you ever knitted for me. Remember? The sleeves were too long and the back was too short — and you told me I must be the wrong shape, that there was nothing wrong with the jersey?'

Christine smiled, uncertainly, and then she couldn't smile any longer.

'I don't remember,' she said, forlornly.

His arm was around her for a moment, holding her close to him.

'Don't worry,' he said, gently. 'These things can't be rushed.' He whistled, and a collie dog came running round the corner of a barn.

'Jess — Jess!' Christine called, delighted, the name out before she had time to think about it.

The dog stood quite still, her ears flat. Then, with a low whine of recognition, she came to Christine.

'You see?' Neil said, not quite steadily. 'It's there, Christine — it's all there, just beneath the surface. It will come.'

He led the way along the path at the back of the barn, and Christine followed him, the dog running ahead of them.

'The boys are working in the barn,'

he told her, casually, 'we'll look in and see them later. Feel up to helping me with afternoon surgery later?'

Panic filled Christine.

'I don't know what to do,' she said, her voice low.

'Yes, you do,' Neil replied, easily. 'You always help me.' He took her hand and swung it gently. 'I told you ten years ago you'd have to work hard, and you said you didn't mind. That still goes.'

He kept her gloved hand in his, easily, casually. And when they reached the top of the hill, and looked back down at the Big House, his eyes met hers and held them, so that once again Christine knew she was blushing. All at once awkward and embarrassed, to be standing here with a man she couldn't remember knowing, and his eyes dark as they looked into hers, she drew her hand away and turned from him, speaking quickly, breathlessly, about the view, about the village in the distance, anything to stop herself from thinking of this strange breathlessness that came over her when this man looked at her.

'Chris,' Neil Ferguson said, gently. 'Stop it — don't panic.'

She looked at him, wordless now.

'Listen, love — I told you what you wanted to know last night because you asked me, because you would have worried more if you hadn't known.'

Christine could feel her heart thudding against her ribs, and she couldn't look away from him.

'Chris, I love you and you love me,' he told her, quietly. 'We have loved each other for a long time — for many years. You may think you have forgotten that, but you haven't. You will remember how we feel about each other, Chris, I promise you that. But — until you do, forget what I said to you last night, what I told you. No — I don't really mean that. Just put it to the back of your mind. I will not mention it again, I will neither say nor do anything that will embarrass you, until you know this and remember it for yourself. But — I will be waiting, Chris.'

175

He turned, then, and strode back down the hill, the dog at his heels. Christine watched him for a moment, warm with gratitude for his tact and his understanding, and then she followed him.

In the warm kitchen, Maggie had a huge pot of tea, and there were about ten teenage boys there, drinking tea out of big mugs and eating home-made scones. They were all quiet when Christine went in with Neil Ferguson, looking at her. For a moment, panic swept over Christine, and then she saw that this wasn't idle curiousity about her loss of memory, about her going away and then coming back — these boys, most of them, cared about her. It mattered to them that she had been ill and unhappy, and they were glad that she had come back.

Neil took her round them, introducing them easily, casually, mentioning that she knew this one, or mentioning that another boy was new. It was only later that Christine began to sort out the boys individually, apart from the red-haired and freckled Keith. But even on that first day she saw that two of them stood apart from the others, aloof and somehow sullen. The other boys all called Neil Dr Neil, their voices warm and affectionate. But these two were different. One had a broken arm, in plaster from his wrist to his shoulder, but she could see no signs of what was wrong with the other.

Later in the day, when she went with Neil to the surgery in the village, she asked him about the boys.

'I've had a bit of trouble with them,' he admitted, his dark eyes clouded. 'Ted — the dark one — is the worst. Tony's got a grouch against society, but I think we can sort him out. But Ted worries me.'

'What's wrong with him?' Christine asked.

'Drugs,' Neil replied, briefly, glancing at her. 'I was in two minds about taking him — I have the other boys to think about — but the alternative was an institution. Rightly or wrongly, I felt he stood a better chance with us. I hope I made the right decision.'

He drew the car up outside a cottage near the hotel.

'Chris,' he said gently, and his hand covered hers, warm and reassuring. 'This won't be too hard. I've told the village people that you've been ill, and that they're not to bother you with questions. They're Highlanders — they'll leave you in peace.'

Christine found that he was right. The soft lilting voices asked her how she was, and there was interest in all the faces, but no one pushed her, or made her feel uncomfortable. To her surprise, she found that Neil was right, that she did know what to do. There was a dressing to be changed, and she found herself automatically turning to the sterilizer, knowing where it was. She knew that she had had no nursing experience before coming here, and yet now there was obviously a background of experience on which she could draw.

'Did I take long to learn how to help here?' she asked Neil curiously as they went home in the car.

He shook his head.

'You were very quick,' he told her.

'But I'd had no experience of nursing at all,' Christine said, frowning.

Neil looked at her for a moment.

'Only nursing Jenny when she was ill,' he replied, his voice even.

'Jenny was never ill,' Christine told him. 'Not even when she was teething. She was such an easy baby, and such a healthy little girl.'

'You — saw her when you were in Edinburgh?' Neil asked her.

Christine looked at him, surprised.

'Of course I saw her,' she replied. 'I told you, they wouldn't let me see her at first, because it would have been such a shock to find that she was seventeen years old instead of seven.'

She was quiet, remembering the dreadful moment of shock, remembering how difficult it had been to grasp this, to understand that she had lost for ever these ten years of her life and of Jenny's.

'Chris — ' Neil said, and there was something strange in his voice, something that made her look at him wonderingly. And then he seemed to change his mind.

'Never mind,' he said, but she could feel that the lightness of his voice was forced. 'Come and see how the boys are doing in the barn — I promised them I'd take you in when we came back.'

There was a big paraffin heater burning in the middle of the barn, but even so it was chilly, and the boys wore thick jerseys. Looking at them, at the coarse navy and grey wool, Christine knew that this was the sort of knitting she was used to doing, this was why knitting for Jenny had been so strange to her.

The boys were making furniture. The red-haired Keith was working on a coffee table, sanding it down with care. Another boy — Jim — was making an old-fashioned wooden cradle, complete with rockers, and Christine exclaimed with delight as she saw it. Two of them were working together on a chest of drawers, and another two were oiling some finished tables.

Christine ran her hand over the rough wood of the cradle.

'But it's beautiful,' she said, softly. She turned to Neil. 'Where do you sell them all?'

Briefly, there was hurt in his eyes, and she knew that this was something she should have known, that it was possibly something they had discussed together. But his voice was even when he answered her.

'There's a distributing centre in Edinburgh,' he told her, 'and another in Glasgow. Whatever we make, we plough back here, with a certain amount put in the boys' savings books. Keith here keeps our accounts — he used to help you with them.'

Distressed, Christine looked up at him.

'I'm sorry, Neil,' she whispered, and

she knew that he understood all that she couldn't say. Sorry that I don't remember, sorry that I have to hurt you by asking about all these things that I should know about.

'Can we start on the toys now, Dr Neil?' one of the boys asked as Neil and Christine turned to go out.

'Sure,' Neil replied. 'Just finish off what you're working on and then get going — it's only three weeks till Christmas. Not much time.'

'Time for what?' Christine asked him as they went across to the kitchen door.

'For the Christmas party toys,' he told her. 'We always have a party for all the village kids — and the boys make toys for them.' He hesitated, and then, not looking at her, he said quietly — 'It was your idea, Chris. At the very beginning, you suggested that it might help some of them to think less of themselves, and to begin to think about other people. It was something I hadn't thought of, and you were right. It helped a great deal, and now it's something of an institution. The old boys tell the newer ones about it.' He closed the kitchen door behind them. 'This will be Keith's second Christmas here.'

'Oh, you're back,' Maggie greeted them from her rocking-chair beside the fire, where she was settled with a big pile of socks to darn. 'The kettle's boiling — make some tea, Chris lass — I could do with another cup myself.' She turned to Neil. 'That lad, Neil, that Ted — I'm no' happy about him. He's got a secretive look in his eyes, and it's not doing Tony any good to be with him all the time.'

Neil set out the cups on the white-scrubbed table under the window.

'I know,' he agreed after a moment. 'I think perhaps I've taken on more than I can deal with this time. But what would you have me do, Maggie? Write and tell the probation folks that we can't cope?'

'Oh no,' the old woman returned vigourously. 'No, we'll no' give in that easy. But — just keep your eye on him,

Neil. That's right, Chris, two of sugar for me, and one for Neil.'

Christine, a little startled, looked up from the cups she had been getting ready. Without thinking, she had known how Neil liked his tea, and how Maggie liked hers.

'Some day,' Neil said softly, his hand brushing hers for a moment as he took the cup from her, 'it will all fall into place, and the gap will be gone.'

'Do you think so?' Christine asked him.

He nodded.

'I'm certain of it. Just have patience. It's all we can do.'

The next day she began helping with the toys for Christmas. The boys were making a dolls' house, and Christine helped with the tiny curtains, the bedcovers, the little rugs on the floors. And there were doll's beds, each with a doll inside, and her job, the boys told her, was always to make dresses for the dolls. In the evening, she and Neil sat in the small study, beside the fire, and she knitted or sewed, surprised herself at how she knew what she wanted to do. The boys had a big room up above, with a record-player, and Neil told her that on principle he left them on their own in the evenings.

'They need freedom,' he said. 'I keep them occupied pretty well through the day, but they need some time to be themselves — and to find themselves sometimes too.'

Maggie liked to go to bed early, and so most evenings they were alone, in the small shabby study. Often, sitting there, Christine would have a groping remembrance, a recognition that she couldn't quite grasp, that eluded her when she tried, of many evenings when they had sat there together, the two of them, in the years gone by.

She had told Neil nothing of what had happened in Edinburgh, nothing of things Valerie had been trying to do. Valerie — and Adam, too. She knew that because of not telling him, she was building up the barrier there was between them, rather than breaking it down, but the shock and the hurt were too recent, too raw, for her to be able to talk of it.

She tried not to think of Jenny, of how she had been at the end, when the dog had been run over. But it was there, in her mind, and sometimes she couldn't avoid it. She knew that this was something she could never forgive either Valerie or Adam for — that either or both of them had deliberately let Jenny be hurt like that because of what they wanted.

Sometimes, when she sat at night thinking of these things, she would look up and find Neil's eyes on her, thoughtful, sympathetic, and she would be tempted to tell him. But in spite of her instinctive warm response to this man, he was still a stranger.

A stranger, she knew, whom she had loved, whom she had promised to marry. But yet, until she could remember this for herself, still a stranger. Until this gap in her life had closed, until the knowledge of her complete relationship with Neil Ferguson was once again part of her known and remembered experience, she couldn't be completely free and open with him, she couldn't look on him as anything but a stranger.

She knew that this hurt and saddened him, and yet she knew too that he understood, that he was prepared to accept her reserve.

But there would be no indefinite putting-off of any decision. Quite apart from what she knew now about Neil and herself, leaving that aside, there was the decision she had already made, to give Adam his freedom. At the time, she had decided to wait until the question of Jenny could be more easily worked out, but since then so many things had changed, because of what Valerie had done.

Christine realized, with pain, that she had lost all the ground she had gained with Jenny. Sometimes she thought of writing to her, of telling her how it had been. But she wasn't certain that the letter would ever reach Jenny, and she wasn't certain how Jenny would receive it. She would still be bitter and resentful, and not prepared to listen to anything her mother had to say.

On an impulse, Christine wrote to John Scott, telling him that he had been right, that she did belong here in Tormore, but that she still could remember nothing more. At the end, she asked him if he would let her know how Jenny was.

A week later, there was a reply from him. His handwriting was bold and slanted and distinctive. He said that he was delighted that she had come to the right place, and that he hoped that soon the once-familiar surroundings would help her to remember completely.

And then, cautiously, he said that Jenny was well, but he felt that she was extremely unhappy.

'Would you give me your permission to do what I think is best if I feel the need arises?' he asked at the end.

The careful wording nevertheless

alarmed Christine. She wrote back immediately to say that of course he must do what he thought best, and would he please let her know if anything else turned up.

Her heart ached for Jenny, but she knew that she dare not go back to the house in Edinburgh.

'Why did it take me so long to decide to ask Adam for a divorce?' Chris asked Neil once. It was something she had wondered about more and more.

Neil hesitated.

'Don't say if you'd rather not,' Christine said quickly, awkwardly, warm colour flooding her cheeks, all at once afraid of what he might say.

'For the first few years that you were here,' Neil told her, his eyes dark as he looked down at her, 'you were — very bitter. I think you had been hurt so badly that you weren't prepared to trust any man, for a long time. And even afterwards, after you turned to me, you always said that you would never give him his freedom.'

Christine looked at him, confused. Give Adam his freedom? Had there been any question of Adam wanting his freedom — then?

'I went away,' Neil told her slowly. 'I went away because I loved you and I wanted to marry you. I stayed away for two years, Chris. When I came back, you — '

He hesitated, and Christine waited, her breath coming unevenly.

'When I came back,' Neil said, not quite steadily, 'you came to meet me in Fort William, and you said that you knew that I was right. That was when you said you would marry me, Chris.'

That strange, inexplicable feeling of remembered happiness when she heard the ship's siren, when she thought of the harbour in Fort William. That was what she had been remembering. Or — remembering without remembering.

'I wish I could remember properly, Neil,' Christine said shakily.

He looked down at her, unsmiling, for a long time.

She wasn't conscious of either of them moving, but the next moment she was in his arms, his lips hard and demanding on hers.

'I'm sorry, Chris,' he said, his voice low, when he let her go at last. 'I shouldn't have done that.'

'Don't be sorry, Neil,' she whispered. She looked up at him, and smiled. 'I think maybe you should have done it sooner.'

For a moment, he looked down at her, surprised. Then, with a sudden shout of laughter, he pulled her close again, and now his lips were warm and tender.

'Get on with your work, woman,' he said when he let her go. 'And let me get on with mine, without these distractions.'

Then, suddenly, he was serious.

'Don't make it too hard for me, Chris,' he said, gravely. 'I've waited so long for you.'

'I'll try not to,' she replied, moved more than she wanted to be by the dark seriousness of his eyes on her face.

A few days before Christmas, the party for the village children was held. Maggie, with Christine helping her, was busy baking for days before it.

'It's a great thing for them, Chris,' she explained, deftly shaping mince-meat pies from the pastry she had made. 'Tormore is such a quiet wee place, with never anything going on, that they look forward to it for a long time. She looked up at Christine, kindness in her bright eyes. 'You always enjoyed it too, lass — and you will this year. Last year — ' she hesitated, and then, not looking at Christine, steadily rolling out the pastry, she went on — 'Last year it was grand. Neil was back, after two years away, and the two of you were so happy.'

How could I have been so happy, Christine thought, sadly, and forget it. How could my mind decide to blank out such happiness?

It seemed to her that it must have

been a different person who could do such a thing, a different person from this Christine, who looked and felt so much better, so much happier, since coming back to the Big House and Neil.

Just as it seemed that it must have been a different person who walked out on Jenny and on Adam ten years ago. Now, there was this new confusion, this worry about whether Neil was right when he said that Adam had wanted a divorce. This was beyond Christine's understanding. But there was nothing she could do about it, no way of finding out whether this was true or not, and so, resolutely, she put it out of her mind, and tried to think only of the Christmas party.

The boys were clearing and decorating the barn, and half an hour before the children were to arrive, Christine and Neil went across to see it. They had cut down and decorated a tree, and they had hung gay streamers around. The big kitchen table had been carried across, and Maggie had just finished setting it.

'But where's the manger?' Christine asked, unthinkingly. And when she had said it, her eyes met Neil's: For she had known, with complete and unquestioning certainty, that they always had a manger under the tree, a manger that one of the first boys they had had, had made for them, years ago.

'Do you remember Steve?' Neil asked, his eyes on her face, intent, a light of hope gleaming in them.

Christine shook her head.

'No,' she admitted, 'it was just — I just knew we always had a manger there.'

'Steve was hurt in a gang fight in Glasgow,' Neil told her. 'His face was slashed. He had plastic surgery, but he needed more than that. I brought him here. You did a lot for him, Christine. He carved the manger for you, just before he left us. He's kept in touch with us, occasionally, through the years, and a couple of months ago we had a

194

letter from him. He's married now, and he and his wife have just had a little girl. He wanted to tell us that they've called her Joy Christine, and — he asked if he could have the manger, for her first Christmas.'

'He called her after me?' Christine asked, wonderingly.

Neil nodded.

'You were the one who got through to him, Chris — I couldn't. He's never forgotten that.' He smiled, then, and touched her cheek lightly, lovingly. 'But that's why we haven't a manger any more.'

'Who did the tiny beds for the dolls' house?' Christine asked the boys. 'It was you, wasn't it, Ted?'

The dark, withdrawn boy shrugged, not rudely, not insolently, but with a cool reserve that Christine found disconcerting.

'Couldn't you do a manger for us?' she asked, ignoring his lack of interest.

'Why should I?' he asked. 'I don't go for mangers.'

'Perhaps you don't,' Christine agreed pleasantly, 'but you're good at carving these tiny things.'

She left it, then, for the first of the children were arriving, their cheeks rosy with the cold, their eyes bright with anticipation. There weren't many of them, for Tormore was such a small village, but this meant that each child was given a present that was just right for him or her. The small boys were given wooden trains, with carriages, and the small girls were given cots with dolls. The dolls' house went to a family of three little girls, and when their father came to take them home, they ran to him.

'Look what they are after giving us,' the eldest said breathlessly.

'Look at the wee beds for the dolls,' the little blonde one told her father.

'It's beautiful just,' the smallest one whispered, touching the tiny gingham curtains.

When they had all gone, the boys finished off the food, and Neil and

Christine left them to clear the barn, and to bring the Christmas tree into the house. Maggie refused any help for the dishes, telling them that Keith and Jim had already volunteered to do them.

Christine made some tea, and they went through to the little study, where the collie, Jess, looked up from the rug in front of the fire and wagged her tail welcomingly.

'Only three days till Christmas,' Neil reminded her as she poured tea for them.

Christine was silent, thinking how strange it was that the last Christmas she could remember was over ten years ago, when Jenny was just seven. They had given her a doll's pram, that year, and Valerie had given her a beautiful new doll. But the small Jenny, her face absorbed, had carefully set the new doll on a chair, and put in the pram instead an old rag doll that Christine had made for her years before.

All the Christmases since then,

Christine thought, with sudden over-whelming sadness, all these years of her childhood that I've missed, that I've lost for ever.

'Don't cry, love,' Neil said, gently, and she tried to say that she wasn't crying, but all the time the tears ran down her cheeks. Haltingly, she tried to explain to him.

'I just keep thinking of Jenny, that last Christmas, and all these years when I wasn't there, and I've lost these years, and they can never come back again,' she said, confusedly. 'And I still don't know how I could ever have gone away and left Jenny.'

'Chris,' Neil said then, with sudden decision, 'there's something I've got to tell you — something about Jenny.'

'About Jenny?'

She looked at him, startled, but before he could say any more the phone rang, shrilly, imperiously. Neil answered, and after a moment he handed it to Christine.

'It's John Scott,' he said, quietly.

'Mrs Lawrence? Christine?' John Scott's voice came over the line clearly, the voice of a man accustomed to giving orders. 'I'm on my way to you in Tormore. I have Jenny with me — I'm bringing her to you. We're in Fort-William — we'll be with you in two hours.'

He rang off, and Christine put the receiver down, dazed.

'What is it?' Neil asked.

'He's coming here,' she told him. 'And he's bringing Jenny!'

Neil took both her hands in his.

'Listen, Chris,' he said, urgently. 'There's something far wrong, something I can't begin to understand. At first I thought you were — imagining things, perhaps, when you talked of Jenny. But if John Scott is coming here and bringing her here — then I don't understand what has happened.'

'What do you mean?' Christine whispered, her lips stiff.

His hands tightened on hers, and his dark eyes looked down into hers.

'Chris, love,' he told her steadily, 'ten years ago, when you came here, you told me that you had left home because your husband was in love with someone else, and wanted a divorce, and — '

He hesitated, and Christine waited, her heart thudding unevenly.

'And because your little girl Jenny was dead,' he said, quietly.

6

'Because Jenny was dead?' Christine repeated, stunned. 'I left Adam because he wanted a divorce, and — because Jenny was dead?'

'That's what you told me,' Neil replied steadily, his dark eyes concerned.

'I must have been out of my mind,' Christine whispered shakily. And what she had just said echoed through her head. Out of my mind, she had said. Had Valerie been right? Had she really been innocent of the things Christine had thought she had done?

'Wait a minute, Chris,' Neil said roughly. 'Don't panic. Let's talk about it, see what we can find out.' He poured another cup of tea for her, hot and strong and sweet. 'Now — what are your last memories and impressions of Jenny and — of him, before you left.

Who was he in love with?'

Christine closed her eyes for a moment, trying to still the whirling confusion of her thoughts.

'Try, Chris,' Neil's voice was low, urgent.

'I don't think Adam was in love with — with Valerie then,' Christine said, slowly, trying to find some sense in the whole thing. 'We were — reasonably happy together. I think I would have known if he had changed.' She looked up at him, her eyes troubled. 'And Jenny had never had a day's sickness in her life.'

'You told me about nursing her,' Neil reminded her, gently. 'She had polio, and she was very ill — you said that you had nursed her until you could do nothing more, and they insisted on taking her to hospital. You collapsed then, with sheer exhaustion, I think, and — when you recovered, Jenny was dead.'

In the familiarity of the shabby little room, what he had said was even more frightening, even less able to be understood.

Then Christine remembered something.

'Valerie told me,' she said, slowly, trying to get it straight in her mind, 'that although I was thinking of Jenny as just seven, in fact she was nearly eight when I — went away. So I don't even remember right up to the time I left them.'

'That's it.' Neil leaned forward, eagerly, his dark eyes alight. 'Look, Chris, I'm only an ordinary GP, this is right out of my line, but this is how I see it. When you reached Edinburgh, something — we may never know what — made your mind decide to blank out these last ten years. But minds are funny things — I don't want to go all psychological and start referring to your subconscious, but in fact that's what it is. Something in you took fright, and decided it didn't want to know anything about the last ten years, it decided to go right back to the time when everything

203

was all right. You and Adam had no problems, your marriage was reasonably happy, and — Jenny was there, alive, a happy little girl of seven who had never had a thing wrong with her. Not a child who had had polio.'

'I can understand that,' Christine agreed, slowly. Then she looked up at him, and now she couldn't hide her distress. 'But Neil, Jenny is alive, there's nothing wrong with her, why should I have said that she was dead?'

Neil shook his head.

'I can't answer that, love,' he said quietly. 'There's something very strange somewhere.' He paused, his dark brows drawn down. 'I can only think, Chris, that you said Jenny was dead, because you thought that she was. Beyond that, I can't take it.' He looked at her, for a moment the doctor taking over from the man. 'And I don't think you should try to take it any further either — at least not now.' He stood up. 'Let's go and get rooms ready for Jenny and for John Scott. Maggie's in bed, but we'll fill hot-water bottles — the two small rooms are always ready anyway.'

For the next two hours, he kept Christine busy, hurrying from one room to another, filling bottles, getting beds ready, lighting fires in the rooms, heating up soup. And Christine was glad to be so busy that she couldn't think, couldn't let her mind dwell on the strange disturbing things she had learned.

It took John Scott longer than the two hours he had estimated, and there was snow on his car when it drew up.

'Came through a blizzard,' he explained, briefly, 'right in the pass. Coming this way, I should think.'

All at once Christine's heart was in her mouth, as he turned to help Jenny out of the car. In spite of everything, she thought, thankfully, Jenny has come to me. No matter what she said before, she has still come to me.

Before Jenny could come out, there was a flurry of movement in the car, and the golden labrador, Guy, jumped out, greeting Christine and Neil with equal enthusiasm and warmth.

'Had to bring him,' John Scott said. 'She wouldn't come without him.'

And then Jenny was there, at the foot of the steps.

'Jenny — Jenny darling,' Christine said, unsteadily, and she ran down and took the girl in her arms. 'Oh, Jenny, you don't know how good it is to see you.'

But Jenny was still and unresponsive in her arms, unyielding.

'I had nowhere else to come to,' she said, sullenly. 'It was Mr Scott who made me come here, when I — when I couldn't stay at home any longer.'

Christine's arms dropped, and she turned to John Scott, bewildered, hurt beyond words.

'We're cold and hungry, Mrs Lawrence — Christine. Can you give us something to eat?' he asked. He held out his hand to Neil. 'Good to see you again, Ferguson.'

Christine understood that he meant

that she was to ask no questions for the moment, and she turned and led the way into the house, Jenny beside her, and the dog running excitedly ahead of them. The kitchen was warm, and she lifted big bowls of soup for the travellers.

'I'm not hungry,' Jenny said sulkily.

'You must eat something, Jenny,' Christine told her, anxiously, looking at the white face and the shadowed eyes. 'Please try to eat some.'

'I'm not hungry,' Jenny repeated, stubbornly.

'Fine,' Neil said easily. 'We'll put it back in the pot then.'

But as he lifted the plate, Jenny mumbled something about eating a little. Christine avoided looking at her, turning to John Scott to ask him about the roads and about their journey. When she did have a quick glance at her daughter, the soup plate was empty, and there was a little colour in Jenny's cheeks.

'I think you should get to bed, Jenny,'

John Scott said brusquely, but not unkindly. 'I'm going to have another cup of tea, if I may. What about taking Jenny to her room, Christine? Plenty time to talk tomorrow.'

Christine understood the guarded advice, and she led Jenny along the corridor and upstairs, with the dog following them.

'The bed should be warm,' she said, carefully keeping her voice light, unquestioning, easy. 'Guy can sleep on the rug beside the fire.' She looked at the small suitcase. 'Got everything you need? Then I'll say goodnight, Jenny — see you in the morning.'

It wasn't easy, but she forced herself to turn and go out of the room, leaving the girl, although everything in her ached to take Jenny in her arms, to break through the sullen reserve and find out what had made Jenny look like this.

In the kitchen, John Scott was talking to Neil, but they both turned round when she went in.

'What happened?' Christine asked unsteadily, her careful control slipping now that Jenny wasn't there. 'Was it because of the dog — because she still thinks I let them out?'

John Scott seemed to know all about the dog.

'No, I don't think so,' he replied, thoughtfully. 'Just after you left, I went to see Jenny. Did it through young Clive — his mother's a cousin of mine. She was still upset about the dog — even told me you had left the gate and the two dogs had got out. But in a week or two, she seemed to be adjusted to that. I managed to see her a few times — had a quiet word with Clive, too, he's got a lot of sense for a young fellow. Then today Clive rang me — asked if he could bring Jenny to me. She was in a bad state — hysterical at first. Wouldn't even see her father. I didn't tell her where I was bringing her until we were almost here.' He smiled, apologetically, but his blue eyes were concerned as they rested on Christine's face.

'She seemed to feel that although she wasn't keen on coming to you, it was the lesser of two evils.'

Neil made an involuntary movement, and John Scott turned to him.

'I must say that, Neil,' he said, gravely. 'It would be cruel and unkind to have Christine hoping for too much, because Jenny has come to her. You must accept that if she had had anywhere else to go, she wouldn't have agreed to come here to you.' He shrugged. 'But she didn't. All we can hope for is that you can break through, find out what the trouble is.'

'What about — about Adam?' Christine asked, forcing herself to keep her voice level and calm. 'Surely he won't let her go like this?'

The older man frowned.

'I can't quite understand this,' he admitted, troubled. 'Adam has always been a little strange about Jenny — wouldn't take her to anything official, wouldn't let her be photographed with him, nothing. Kicked up such a fuss once when Jenny won a cup for swimming, insisted her picture wasn't to go in the paper. Yet now, after all these years of what he calls protecting Jenny — when I rang to say that she seemed to be upset about something, that I was taking her off to spend a few weeks with some relatives — I didn't say whether my relatives or hers! — he didn't object.'

'He would if he knew she was coming to me,' Christine pointed out. She hesitated and then, carefully, asked John Scott if Adam had said anything about her.

'I asked about you,' the older man told her. 'Gave him a week to volunteer information, then I asked where you were — had to drop in to see him about some committee meeting.'

He hesitated, and Christine waited.

'I don't know quite how to say this,' he said at last, troubled. 'And I mustn't risk giving you the wrong impression. He didn't in so many words say this, but undoubtedly, if I hadn't known

211

exactly where you were, I would have thought — he said that you hadn't been well, that there seemed to be delayed effects of the concussion, and — and he said that the doctor felt that some treatment was necessary.'

Anger flushed Christine's cheeks, but she didn't say anything.

'If I hadn't known,' John Scott said again, reluctantly, 'I would certainly have thought that you were in a nursing-home somewhere, and that the only decent thing to do was to ask as little as possible about the whole thing.'

'What is this all about, Chris?' Neil asked, and she could see that he was hurt because she had told him nothing of this.

John Scott stood up.

'I'm tired,' he said abruptly. 'Have to leave early tomorrow morning — have you got a bed for me tonight, Christine?'

Christine took him upstairs, where the fire was blazing brightly in the hearth.

'Haven't seen a real patchwork quilt since my mother died,' he said, touching Maggie's quilt, admiringly. He turned to Christine. 'He's a fine, straight man, Neil Ferguson,' he said, abruptly. 'Don't hold anything back from him. You've got to get this whole thing sorted out — he can't help unless you tell him the lot.'

Slowly, almost reluctantly, Christine went back down to the kitchen. Neil was standing with his back to the fire, waiting for her. She could see that he was angry, angry and hurt.

'I'm sorry, Neil,' she said slowly, unhappily. 'I should have told you everything, but — it wasn't easy.'

Some of the cold anger left his eyes.

'Sit down beside me, Chris,' he told her, 'and let's have it.'

She sat down on the old couch beside him, and then, carefully, trying to leave nothing out, she told him everything that she had kept back until now. The confusion about the tins of food, the sleeping pills. And the unlatched gate

213

that had let Jenny's dogs run out, and had caused the death of one of them. And Valerie and Adam — together.

Then, not looking at him, she told him of what Valerie had said when she said that she intended telling the doctor at the hospital everything that had happened.

'That was when I gave up, Neil,' she said at last, tiredly. 'Maybe it was foolish, maybe the doctor would have believed me, but — I wasn't seeing things straight by then, all I knew was that I had to get away.'

'Why didn't you tell me this, love?' Neil asked her, and although his voice was gentle, although his arm around her was steady and reassuring, she saw that his eyes were dark and bleak.

'I don't know,' Christine admitted, leaning back against him. 'I wanted to, but — ' She looked up at him, admitting the truth for the first time even to herself. 'I think, Neil, I was afraid that you might think so too — that you might feel that I'd been imagining things. And if you did, then — the logical thing would be to agree with what Valerie said, that I needed some — treatment, that I was neurotic and unbalanced.'

'You're no more neurotic and unbalanced than I am, love,' Neil assured her, and the conviction in his voice brought unexpected tears to her eyes. Then he looked down at her, and his eyes were troubled. 'But I have to admit that if you'd told me this before — when I thought you were only imagining that Jenny was alive, that you had seen her — I don't know how I would have taken it then.' He straightened up. 'There's a lot to be sorted out, Chris,' he told her, deliberately, 'and too much has happened now. I wanted to wait until there were some signs that your memory was returning — I thought the familiarity of everything here would help. But I don't think we can wait, I think we must do something right away.'

'Not right away,' Christine reminded

him. 'There's Jenny. We must try to sort out what has happened with her, before we start on anything else.'

They talked about it, and after a while Neil agreed, reluctantly, to give it a few days and to see what the position with Jenny was, before doing anything. When Christine at last went to bed, she was exhausted — too tired to sleep. For the first time since coming back to the Big House, she lay restless, thoughts going round and round in her mind, possible explanations coming to her and then being rejected.

It was almost morning when she at last fell asleep, and she awoke tired and unrefreshed. John Scott looked at her shrewdly when he came into the kitchen.

'You've been worrying, Christine,' he accused her.

She tried to smile.

'It's difficult not to,' she replied. 'There's so much that I just don't understand.'

She gave him some breakfast, and sat

down with a cup of tea beside him. Maggie was having what she called a 'long lie', which meant that she'd get up about eight instead of seven. Jenny was still asleep. Christine had opened the door softly and looked in. There were tear-smudges on Jenny's cheeks, and just for a moment, watching her, Christine had seen another fleeting resemblance to the small Jenny.

'What don't you understand, lass?' the older man asked, and the unexpected kindness in his voice brought a blur of tears to Christine's eyes.

She shook her head, for there was too much to tell him, too much to grasp all at once.

'Adam and Valerie, for one thing,' she said after a moment. 'I — don't remember, but it seems as if they were in love with each other even before I left Adam — Neil says that I told him Adam wanted a divorce, but I wasn't prepared to give him one.' She looked up at John Scott. 'I don't like divorce, but surely that was very hard and unforgiving of me?'

'I don't know, Christine,' he replied, answering the bewilderment in her voice. 'There could be circumstances that change the way it looks.'

Christine handed him two slices of freshly-done toast, and some farm butter.

'And there's another thing,' she said, slowly. 'All the time I was away — why didn't Adam either divorce me for desertion, or have me presumed dead? Then he could have married Valerie.'

'I can't say any more than I did before,' John Scott replied, after a moment. 'Divorce is not a good thing for a man in Adam's position, in spite of changing times, and permissive societies.' He shook his head. 'No, I can't explain that, but this I can say.'

Christine looked up at the sudden vigour in his voice.

'I've heard people discussing Adam,' he told her. 'And I've heard them say what a wonderful person he is, to be so loyal to a wife whom most people assumed had just walked out on him for no reason at all. This doesn't lose him any votes, Christine — but a divorce might have.'

'But Valerie?' Christine asked, frowning. 'Would she be content with things like that?'

He shrugged.

'I can't say. But I do know that the impression I have of her is that she's a woman with the patience to wait for what she wants.' His blue eyes held hers. 'Next year,' he told her, 'I think Adam will get in to Parliament. Now let's look at it this way. After he was in, if there was still no sign of you I think it's possible that he might have decided — regretfully, of course — that his loyalty had been stretched far enough, that he would have to give in.'

'But I did turn up,' Christine reminded him.

He looked at her.

'Yes, and if things had gone the way they looked, with Adam hinting that perhaps some of the time you were away had been spent in a mental home, hinting too that you were anything but fully recovered — well, it's a situation in which his constituents would have felt every sympathy with him. I don't think he would have lost any votes then, either.'

He frowned.

'Getting old,' he told her abruptly. 'There's some thought round the corner of my mind, and I can't get hold of it, something I should remember. No — no use.' He stood up. 'Time I was on my way. Say goodbye to Jenny for me, and to Neil Ferguson, he was out early, I heard him leave.' He hesitated. 'If you come to Edinburgh for any reason, come and stay with me. I rattle about in my house now that my wife's dead and my sons both in Canada. I might be able to help you, too, I've got quite a few contacts.'

His blue eyes were bright under the white brows.

'Kiss me goodbye, Christine,' he said, smiling. 'It's a privilege I think I have the right to claim now.'

Christine kissed him, and his hand gripped hers for a moment.

'Chin up, lass,' he said, gruffly. 'And don't just sit down under all this — do something about it.'

He had gone before Maggie came down, and Christine told the old woman that Jenny was there. For a moment, there was the same blank astonishment in Maggie's eyes that there had been in Neil's, then, quickly, she turned away.

'That's nice for you,' she said, bending down to pick a spoon up from the floor. 'Does Neil know?'

'Maggie,' Christine said gently, 'it's all right. Neil told me that I said Jenny was dead, when I came here ten years ago. I — I don't know why I said that, I don't know why I thought it, but I do know this.' And the knowledge had come to her slowly, through the long sleepless night. 'I would never, never have left Jenny. No matter what Adam had done, no matter how unhappy I was, I would never have left Jenny. But — if she was dead, if I thought she was dead — ' She shook her head, trying to clear the heaviness left from her lack of sleep. 'I still can't understand it, but I do know that I would never have left her.'

She turned back to the cooker.

'I'm going to take her up some breakfast,' she said, trying to talk and move briskly. She hesitated, and then, carefully, told Maggie a little of how things were between Jenny and her, of Jenny's resentment and feeling that if she had had anywhere else to go she would have gone anywhere rather than to her mother.

'Don't you go running after her, then,' Maggie advised. 'Take her a cup of tea and tell her she'll get breakfast in the kitchen when she's ready.'

A little reluctantly, Christine did this. Jenny was just waking up, her fair hair tousled, her eyes still sleepy, but clearer than they had been the night before, Christine saw with relief.

'Tea now, Jenny,' she said, forcing herself to speak briskly, pleasantly but coolly. 'Come down to the kitchen and have something to eat.' She hesitated. 'Did Mr Scott tell you anything about the house — about Tormore?'

'A little,' Jenny said grudgingly. 'He said you have boys here who need medical care and also need help in other ways. He — he said you had done a lot for the boys, you and Dr Ferguson.'

She didn't look at her mother while she made the reluctant admission. But Christine, taking a chance, sat down on the edge of the bed.

'And you feel it doesn't matter how much I've done for them, I should have been with you? Is that it?'

Jenny looked back at her, hostility tinged with surprise at Christine's direct attack.

'I'm still no nearer knowing what happened, Jenny,' Christine admitted. She was reluctant to say anything to Jenny about having presumably thought that she was dead. 'And — to the end of my life, I'll never stop regretting these ten lost years when I didn't have you. You must believe that.' She stood up. 'And you must believe, too, that I did shut the dogs in. I don't know what happened, but — Jenny, I would never have let anything happen to your dogs.'

The girl said nothing, and after a moment Christine went out, thinking unhappily that perhaps there should have been a better way of doing this, some way that would have convinced Jenny. But she couldn't tell her anything of what Adam and Valerie had done, it was too much of a burden to put a girl who wasn't even eighteen yet.

A little later Jenny came down for breakfast, the golden labrador at her heels. The collie, Jess, was suspicious at first, but when Christine sat down on the floor and talked to the two dogs together, she was prepared to accept them, and a little while later, Christine saw that she had moved along the hearthrug to make room for him.

'Look, Jenny,' she said, softly. 'They've made friends.'

'More than you've done,' old Maggie put in unexpectedly. 'I haven't seen a smile since you came in to the room, and your mother that pleased to have you here.'

'Maggie, please just leave it,' Christine said quickly, uneasily.

Maggie sniffed.

'Manners is manners, that's what I say,' she said to no one in particular. 'Here — I'll wash these and you can dry up for me, then your mother will take you over to say hello to the boys. After this you can get up in time to give me a hand with breakfast for them.'

Amused in spite of herself, Christine saw the surprise in Jenny's blue eyes.

When the dishes were finished, Christine took her across to the barn, and introduced her to the boys.

'This is my daughter, Jenny,' she said, and then went round the boys in turn.

'Hi, Jenny,' Keith said enthusiastically. 'We're glad to have you here.'

Then he blushed to the roots of his red hair.

'Hi,' Jenny returned, without any enthusiasm.

'You should see the lovely furniture the boys make, Jenny,' Christine said. 'And if only you'd been here yesterday, you could have seen the toys. You'd have loved the dolls' house.' She turned to Keith. 'I wonder if I could take her to the Macraes' house and ask to see it?'

'Mrs Macrae would be pleased,' the boy agreed.

'Look at this, Jenny,' Christine said, pointing out the hinged wooden work-basket Ted was working on. He had ignored her suggestion of making a manger, and she didn't want to push it. 'Isn't this beautiful?'

Jenny shrugged.

'I suppose so,' she agreed, indifferently.

Suddenly, to her own surprise, Christine was furious with her daughter.

'Look, Jenny,' she said, more loudly

than she had meant to, 'I'm sorry for — for everything that has happened, and I know you've got a chip on your shoulder. But you're not taking it out on my boys.' She turned back to Ted, just in time to see a spark of interest in the usual reserve of his face. 'Let me know when you want that lined, Ted,' she told him crisply, 'and I'll find some material.'

She walked out then, with Jenny behind her. And outside the barn, she turned to the girl.

'I'll say this once, Jenny,' she told her quietly. 'You are not taking out your grudges on these boys. They've had a tough time, all of them, in different ways, and Neil has done wonders with them. I will not have you undoing the good he has done, so you might as well accept that from the start.'

The girl looked at her, startled.

'Sorry,' she mumbled, indistinctly, after a moment.

Christine knew that the grudging apology was all she was likely to get, so she left things there.

'Let's take the dogs out,' she suggested, 'if Maggie doesn't need any help. I'm on at the surgery this afternoon, but we can take them out for half an hour now.'

They walked up the hill, neither of them saying anything, although at the top Christine pointed out the village, far beneath them, and Loch More in the distance, at the far side of the hill, or tor.

'And there — that cottage at the far end of the village — that's Neil's surgery,' she said.

And turning to Jenny, she saw something in the girl's face that stopped her:

'Jenny?' she whispered, uncertainly. 'What is it?'

But Jenny turned away from her.

'Nothing,' she said coolly, the reserve in her voice shutting Christine out.

Christine put her hand on Jenny's arm, and the instant, involuntary withdrawal made her catch her breath.

But in spite of this hostility, she felt that if she didn't go on now, she might never find out what had made Jenny leave home.

'Jenny,' she began, trying to keep her voice steady, 'tell me why you left home.'

Jenny shrugged.

'Probably the same reason you did,' she replied, and Christine, listening to her and loving her with an aching intensity, could hear the bewilderment underneath the flippancy of her voice.

'Why do you think I did?' she asked.

Jenny's blue eyes met hers for a moment, and then the girl turned away, looking out across the snow-topped mountains.

'Because you found out what I did — that Aunt Valerie and — and my father are having an affair.'

Somehow, the deliberate sophistication of the phrase she had used told Christine just how hurt the girl was — hurt and shocked.

'I don't know that I would put it like

that,' she replied, as casually as possible. 'The way I see it is that your father has been lonely since I — went away ten years ago. He and Valerie have quite naturally fallen in love with each other.'

No need to say to Jenny, she decided quickly, that it seemed that they had been in love ten years ago, that that could have had something to do with her going away.

Jenny looked at her, curiously.

'You're very generous,' she said, her voice low. Then she shrugged again. 'Of course, why should it matter to you? You have Dr Ferguson, my father has Valerie — all you need to do now is legalize the whole thing.'

'That is what we want to do,' Christine told her steadily.

'So much for marriage,' Jenny commented lightly — too lightly, as they turned to walk back down the hill. 'Just confirms what I told Clive.'

'What did you tell Clive?' Christine asked.

'Just that it seems to me marriage is for the birds,' Jenny told her, and she smiled, but it was a smile that tore at Christine's heart, for there was still hurt bewilderment in Jenny's blue eyes.

'What did Clive think about that?' Christine said then, managing to keep her voice casual.

'Oh, he's old-fashioned,' Jenny replied. 'He believes in marriage and all that sort of thing.' She turned and whistled to the two dogs. 'Just shows how right I am that we've nothing much in common.'

What have we done to you, Jenny, Christine asked herself, unhappily. And is there anything we can do to put things right?

'I didn't leave Edinburgh because of that, Jenny,' she said, determined that now this must all be cleared up. 'I left because I couldn't bear to have you look at me the way you did when you thought the dog died because of my carelessness.'

Jenny stopped, and looked at her.

Christine met the blue eyes steadily. It was true. Although there were the other aspects — the things Valerie and Adam were trying to do — this was what had been the last straw, the final blow.

'You really mean that,' Jenny said, wonderingly, and it wasn't a question. And then, in a moment, the warmth and the light died from her face.

'If you do feel like that,' she asked, and once again there was cool hostility in her voice, 'then why did you walk out on me ten years ago, when I was ill?'

'When you were ill?' Christine repeated, and everything in her was still.

'I had polio,' Jenny said steadily, 'and they took me to hospital. When I came back home — you had gone. Dad — my father had no idea of why you had gone and — neither had I.'

Christine shook her head.

'I'm sorry, Jenny,' she said shakily, 'I still don't know any more about that. I — didn't even know you had been ill. Neil — Dr Ferguson told me that I had told him that when I first met him, ten years ago.'

She was tempted to tell Jenny that it seemed that she had thought that her daughter was dead, but it was too bewildering, too — frightening, almost, in its implications, and she decided to say nothing about that.

'Just tell me this,' Jenny asked her, and Christine's heart ached because Jenny still couldn't address her as Mummy or Mother. 'Did you know Dr Ferguson before you left my father?'

It was what she had wondered herself, so she couldn't, Christine felt, blame Jenny for wondering too.

'No,' she told her with certainty. 'He told me that he met me in Inverness after I had left Adam. I was — very unhappy.'

Jenny looked at her, consideringly, and Christine's heart lifted a little.

'Let's leave it for now, Jenny,' she suggested, as casually as possible. 'We aren't going to get any further.'

'What are you going to do?' Jenny

233

asked her, as they came round the curve of the path in behind the barn. 'I mean — about my father, and about Dr Ferguson?'

'I — don't quite know, Jenny,' Christine replied, slowly. Her instinct was to say that this was something between Neil and her, but Jenny was involved too, she had a right to know. 'We haven't really decided, but — ' She is nearly eighteen, she reminded herself, she is — or was — in love with Clive, she isn't a child. 'It's like this, Jenny,' she said quietly, 'When I came here — when Mr Scott told me how to get here — Neil — Dr Ferguson — told me that I left here to go to Edinburgh and to ask your father for a divorce, so that I could marry him. He — says that he has been in love with me for many years, but that for a long time I wouldn't consider divorce.'

She opened the kitchen door and led the way in, grateful that for once the kitchen was empty, and Maggie elsewhere.

'But this is only something I've been told,' she went on, almost to herself. 'I know it's true, I know Neil is telling me the truth, but — it isn't something that you just accept someone else's word for, and he understands that. We must wait — we have to wait — until I know for myself that this is true, until I accept it for myself. Even if I never remember anything else, I must either remember that, or — or discover it again.'

This was more than she had intended saying, and as Jenny's eyes rested on her Christine felt warm colour rising in her cheeks. I'm thirty-nine, she thought, with some embarrassment, and Jenny is eighteen. I can't expect her to understand something like this.

'I'll make a cup of tea for us,' Jenny murmured awkwardly, brusquely, turning to the kettle on the fire. And Christine realized that this was a big step forward, that perhaps Jenny had understood a little of what she had been trying to say.

'I thought I heard you come in,'

Maggie said, opening the door. 'Tea? Grand, I could just do with a cup. Jenny, would you fill the pot up again, lass, and take it across to the boys? There's some biscuits in that big tin over there.'

Small as Maggie was, it had already dawned on Christine that you didn't argue with her, and Jenny seemed to think the same. Obediently, she did what she was told, and went across the yard with a loaded tray.

'Time she realized there's folks worse off than her,' Maggie remarked, stirring her second cup of tea.

'She — hasn't had a very easy time,' Christine said, defensively.

'No, I'm sure of that,' Maggie agreed, swinging over with disconcerting speed. 'But it seems to me she has the same problem we used to say the lads had, the problem that held up everything, until you came up with the answer. She thinks too much about herself — she'll be a lot better when she begins to think about other folk. But I can see she'll maybe need to get some of her own problems sorted out first.'

Christine stood up, and took her cup across to the sink.

'I — just hope we can sort some of them out,' she said, and all at once the strain of the talk with Jenny began to tell on her.

'Sit down at the fire, Chris, you're tired out,' Maggie said, and the rough kindness in the old woman's voice brought tears to Christine's eyes. 'And you have surgery this afternoon, too. Is that Neil's car now?' She looked out of the kitchen window. 'You just pour a cup of tea for him, lass — I'll go over and see that Jenny's managing with the boys' tea.'

'Where's Maggie hurrying off to?' Neil asked when he came in a moment later.

And in spite of her emotional exhaustion, Christine had to smile.

'She's being tactful,' she told him. 'Haven't you noticed how often she leaves us together, Neil?'

He put down his bag and came over to her, taking both her hands in his.

'You're cold, Chris,' he said, surprised. 'Have you been out?'

She nodded.

'Jenny and I took the dogs to the top of the hill.' She hesitated, and then, while he drank the tea she had poured for him, she told him of her conversation with Jenny, of what Jenny had said about her father and Valerie.

'We might have thought of that,' Neil commented when she had finished. 'What surprises me is why she's noticed nothing in all these years.'

'I should think they've been very careful,' Christine said, her voice low. 'If John Scott is right — if Adam is so afraid for his reputation that he wouldn't risk divorcing me for desertion — then he — they — must have taken great care. And — for so long, Jenny has accepted having Valerie around, she wouldn't think of any other relationship. But — now she's growing up, and beginning to see things differently.'

She looked across at Neil, and now she couldn't hide her distress.

'Do you know what she said, Neil?' she told him, not quite steadily. 'She said to me — So much for marriage. She and this boy, Clive — I know they're both young, but there was something — something rather special between them, Neil. And now — Jenny says she doesn't believe in marriage. She — she says Adam has Valerie and — I have you.'

He came across and sat on the arm of her chair.

'What did you say?' he asked her, gently.

Christine shook her head, forlornly.

'There wasn't much I could say, Neil. I tried to make her see how things are between us, but I don't know — '

'Chris,' he said, and the low urgency of his voice made her face flood with colour. 'Chris — how are things between us?'

She wanted to look away, but his eyes held hers.

'I don't know,' she murmured at last.

She saw the swift disappointment darken his eyes, and instinctively, then, she put out her hand to him.

'Don't look like that, Neil,' she said, shakily. 'I — I said to Jenny that it isn't possible to accept someone else's word for something like this. I have to know for myself that — that I love you.'

'And what if you never remember, Chris? What then?' His voice was hard, and there was a bleakness in his eyes that tore at her heart. And yet, this had to be completely clear between them.

'If I never remember loving you before, Neil,' she said, and now her voice was steady, 'then — then I think I might find myself falling in love with you again.'

The bleakness left his eyes as he looked down at her.

'Am I allowed to help you to do that?' he asked her, and he smiled.

Her reply must have been in her eyes, for he leaned forward and kissed her, his lips warm on her, warm and

— right, somehow, with a dear familiarity that went beyond memory.

'I think,' he said when he released her, 'that you and I must be taking a trip to Edinburgh soon, love. No — don't be afraid. I will be with you every minute of the time, they can do nothing to you.'

'Not yet,' Christine whispered, knowing she was being a coward. 'At least not until after Christmas, Neil.'

'Perhaps not,' he agreed. 'But — we will not wait too long, Chris.' He stood up, then, and pulled her to her feet. 'Are you coming across with me? I must see how the boys are doing.'

Christine lifted her duffle coat from behind the kitchen door. Warm as the beautiful sheepskin-lined coat she had come in was, she felt far more at home in this old one that Maggie told her she had had for years.

They went across the yard, and Neil pointed to the clouds, low and heavy on the hill.

'Looks as if we'll have snow for

Christmas,' he commented.

The barn was warm, and as they went in, Neil murmured to her that there was a great difference in the boys since Jenny came. Keith had an old guitar out, and Jim was singing a folk-song, with Jenny and the other boys humming too. Maggie stood watching them, trying to look disapproving, but not succeeding very well.

Neil held Christine back at the door until the song finished, and then they went forward.

'I liked that, Keith,' he said, warmly. 'Didn't you, Maggie?'

The boys went back to their work, and Jenny picked up the big tray and carried it across to the kitchen.

Maggie sniffed.

'Plenty more to do than that,' she replied. And then, a little unwillingly, 'But you play real nice, Keith, I must say that.' She looked around at the boys. 'This afternoon, I want you all out cutting logs for me — there's snow on the way, and I'm no' wanting us to be caught unprepared. Finish up what you're busy on, and then we'll get logs in. Is that all right with you, Neil?'

'Fine with me, Maggie,' Neil replied. 'Anything you want done, Chris?'

She hesitated, and then, looking at Ted, she asked him if he was going to do a manger to go under the tree.

'I don't go for mangers,' he said, as he had the other day.

Christine would have left it there, but suddenly, surprisingly, Jenny was between them, her blue eyes flashing, her cheeks flushed.

'Don't you speak like that to my mother,' she told him scornfully. 'Just yesterday I heard her call you all her boys. If you can't make a manger just say so — I bet you can't, anyway.'

The childish challenge nevertheless seemed to get through to Ted.

'I can too,' he replied, angrily. He turned to Christine. 'But you didn't mean me when you said my boys.'

'I did, Ted,' Christine replied, steadily, answering the doubt in his eyes. 'As it happens, when I said that to Jenny — it was specially you I meant.'

For a moment, the boy looked at her, and then, briefly, there was a warmth on his face that was almost a smile.

'I'll see what I can do,' he mumbled, and Christine knew she must leave it there.

'What can I do, Maggie?' she asked.

'Run to the end of the road and see if the postie's been,' Maggie suggested. 'That big brute in front of the fire could do with a run, eh Guy?'

The golden labrador rose at the sound of his name, looking eagerly at Jenny. When the door closed behind them, Christine turned to Neil.

'Did you hear that?' she asked him, excitement warming her voice. 'She — she said Don't speak like that to my mother.'

'Good for Jenny,' Neil replied. 'And good for Ted, too. Did you see the way he looked when she said it?'

They talked about the boy, not being too hopeful, but yet feeling that perhaps a breakthrough wasn't too far away. Then Jenny came back with the letters, holding out one to Christine.

'I think it's from Mr Scott,' she said. 'I'm going over to see how the boys are doing.'

Maggie went upstairs, and Christine and Neil were left alone.

'He must have written as soon as he got back to Edinburgh,' Christine commented, opening the letter. 'I suppose he — '

Then a phrase in the letter caught her eyes and she read it. She felt all the colour leave her face as she did what John Scott said, and looked at the photograph that was enclosed.

'Chris — is something wrong?' Neil asked, concerned.

She looked at him, completely shaken.

'Yes, there is,' she said, slowly. 'Neil — John Scott says that Adam knew where I was, that he knew I was here — years ago. He knew, and — he didn't do anything about it.'

245

7

'How did he know that you were here?' Neil asked.

Christine handed him the photograph. It showed Neil, with the group of boys, some of them crippled, some with legs or arms in plasters, working in the barn. And in the background, there was a woman. Herself.

'He says this is what he was trying to think of. About eight years ago, he was here on holiday, and he took this picture, and put a story about the house and the boys in the Star. He was here for such a short time that he wasn't even introduced to me, and my name wasn't there, but — but Adam had seen it in the paper and recognized me.'

She handed Neil the letter, and watched him read it.

'And Adam came into the office and asked to see the original — said he was interested in giving us something. In fact, all he wanted was a closer look at you in the picture.' Neil's mouth was set and grim.

'But why didn't he come and see me?' Christine asked him, bewildered, unable to understand this.

Neil shook his head.

'Why should he?' he asked her. 'He had got what he wanted — you had left him, and he had Valerie.' He put the letter and the photograph down on the table. 'Now, of course, we know why Adam didn't divorce you for desertion or have you presumed dead. Because he knew darned well where you were — and that you were alive. And it would have been very embarrassing indeed if he had started divorce proceedings and you had turned up.'

'But that didn't help him,' Christine pointed out, forcing herself to keep her voice steady. 'He still wanted a divorce . . . '

She told him then what John Scott had mentioned to her about Adam's hopes for a seat in Parliament, about John Scott's idea that until he had achieved this, he dare not risk a divorce.

'Could be,' Neil agreed, but without complete conviction. 'I don't know — I don't think people look quite so badly on divorce, not even in Scotland.' He looked at her, his eyes dark, concerned. 'What really bothers me, Chris, is that he knew where you were, and he kept you and Jenny apart all these years.'

Tears blurred Christine's eyes.

'I don't think I can ever forgive him for that,' she said, her voice low. 'There's still so much I don't understand, but however you look at it, he knew where I was, and he did nothing about it. And nothing can ever give me back these years with Jenny that I've lost.'

'Christmas is the day after tomorrow,' Neil said, with decision. 'If we can, we'll go to Edinburgh between Christmas and New Year, otherwise right after New Year, I'm not suggesting this, love — I'm telling you.'

He looked at his watch.

'I want to go to the head of the glen to see old Archie Macullum,' he told her. 'Then I'll be back for lunch, and we'll go down for surgery.' At the door, he turned. 'I don't think we should say anything about this to Jenny — not yet. Not until we know more clearly what the whole story is.'

Christine agreed, but she was afraid that Jenny might ask what John Scott's letter had been about. But Jenny spent the rest of the morning over at the barn, and she and the boys spent the whole of lunchtime in a heated argument about Women's Lib, Jenny with her eyes bright and her cheeks flushed. When Christine and Neil went out to drive to the village, the boys were starting on the log-gathering Maggie had ordered, and Jenny was helping them, the hood of her duffle coat up over her fair hair, and a pair of old woollen gloves of Maggie's on her hands.

The clouds were lower, and there was

the feeling of snow in the air, as they opened the surgery, and Christine began to sort out the patients' cards. Not many had ventured out today — there was a dressing to be changed, a farmer who had been out shooting rabbits and had fallen, so that his gun had gone off and wounded him in the leg. And there was a checkup on a child who had had his tonsils removed in Fort William a week before, and then an old man who greeted Christine with delighted welcoming.

'It's yourself, nurse,' he said, smiling. 'I heard you were back, and it's grand just to see you again.'

Christine looked at Neil, hoping he would help her.

'Aye, but it's not so grand to see you back here again, Davie,' Neil said, easily. 'Is it that ulcer playing up again?'

'Aye, it is that,' the old man replied, sorrowfully. He looked at Neil, his grey eyes innocent. 'And me treating it like a lord — drinking milk all the time, as if I was a bairn again.'

'But what do you drink in the milk?' Neil asked, and the limpid grey eyes looked away.

'Sure the milk has such a dreadful taste,' the old man admitted after a moment, 'that maybe sometimes — not often, you understand, doctor, just sometimes — I have to put in a wee drop of whisky, just to take the taste away. But surely a wee drop could not be doing any harm?'

'Depends how wee the wee drop is, Davie,' Neil replied, writing out a prescription. 'All right, back on the tablets, and remember, Davie — go easy on the drink at New Year. You'll be sorry if you take too much.'

'Aye, but I'll be sorry too if I don't take any,' old Davie pointed out reasonably, taking the prescription. 'Ah well, we'll just have to do our best, won't we doctor?'

'We will that, Davie,' Neil agreed, smiling.

All through the next day it snowed, and at the Big House there was a feeling of suppressed excitement, of Christmas around the corner. Christine, watching Jenny's bright face, thought with an ache in her throat of all the Christmases with Jenny that she had missed, that she could never have.

There was still a definite constraint in Jenny when she talked to Christine, and yet it seemed to Christine that things were a little easier, that there was less hostility when Jenny looked at her. She told herself that perhaps she was hoping for too much too soon, considering how upset Jenny had been when she arrived. And yet — seeing her with the boys, talking easily and naturally, Christine couldn't help thinking that things might be all right between Jenny and her, given time and patience.

In the evening, the boys invited them up to the big room upstairs. There was always a fire burning, and the old couch was pulled close to it. They all sat near the fire, and Keith played his guitar, playing old Christmas carols, new songs that Jenny and the boys all seemed to know, and familiar folk-songs. Christine and Maggie had made hot fruit punch, spiced with ginger, and they drank big glasses of that.

Once, looking down at Jenny, Christine saw the blue eyes shadowed, and her mouth still, sad.

'Don't, Jenny,' she murmured, leaning forward and touching the girl's shoulder, under cover of the singing. 'Don't let it make you so unhappy.'

Your father isn't worth it, she wanted to say — he kept you and I apart for years, when we could have been together. But Adam *was* Jenny's father, and — there was still the memory of the early years in the cottage, the years when Jenny was a baby, the years when she and Adam were happy together. The years before she went away from them.

'I was thinking about Clive,' Jenny murmured, colouring. 'I — I told him I didn't want to see him again.'

'Have you changed your mind, then?' Christine asked.

'I — don't know,' Jenny admitted. She looked up at her mother, her blue eyes clouded. 'But I miss him more than I thought I would.'

'Jenny — sing us Mary's Boy Child,' Keith called from the other side of the room. 'You sang it this morning.'

Jenny's voice wasn't strong, but it was sweet, a little husky, and the room was silent as she sang, accompanied by the chords from the guitar. When she had finished, there was no sound for a little. And then, faint and distant, there was the sound of the church bells from the village. One of the boys opened the window, and the night air, cold and crisp, carried the sound to them. The snow had stopped, but it was white all around. Not deep, but giving everything a clean, newly-laundered look.

'Happy Christmas, Jenny,' Christine said, not quite steadily, as she thought of all the Christmasses they had been apart, she and Jenny.

Jenny looked back at her, unsmiling.

'Happy Christmas, Mum,' she murmured, awkwardly. Briefly, her soft young lips touched Christine's cheeks, and then she drew back, as if she had done and said more than she had intended to.

Someone suggested cocoa, and they all trooped down to the kitchen. For a moment, Neil and Christine were alone.

'Happy Christmas, love,' Neil said.

He took her in his arms and kissed her. And all at once Christine found herself responding with fierce urgency, clinging to him, so that at last, when they drew apart, she could see that Neil was as shaken as she was.

'It's been long enough, Chris,' Neil murmured, his lips against her hair. 'We've got to get things sorted out.'

'We have,' Christine agreed, slowly. 'Just as soon as we can, Neil.'

He kissed her again, but gently this time, a kiss that was a promise and a pledge. And then they went down to the kitchen to join the others.

The next morning, Christine woke early.

Already there was a great deal of noise from upstairs, where the boys were. Then she heard footsteps on the stairs, and whispering, and a knock on Jenny's door, next to hers.

'I'm coming,' Jenny called, her voice light and clear, and someone outside told her to keep quiet.

Christine, amused, waited until she heard Jenny go out, and go on downstairs with the boys. Then she got up and dressed, quickly, pulling on warm slacks and a thick jersey.

But just as she opened her door they were there, all of them, with Keith balancing precariously a cup of tea on a tray. Christine sat down on her bed to drink it, while two of the other boys took tea in to Neil and to Maggie. Five minutes later Neil appeared, a thick grey polo-neck sweater on, his dark hair rumpled, and his eyes still sleepy.

'You've to come downstairs,' Jenny

told them, excitement flushing her cheeks.

The tree was in the front hall, and they hadn't been allowed to see it the night before, for Jenny and the boys had decorated it. Now they led Christine and Neil up to it. There was a fairy on top, something that hadn't been there when the tree was in the barn.

'Jenny made it,' Keith said, and Jenny coloured.

'We always used to have a fairy on top,' she said defensively. 'But — we haven't for a long time, I thought it would be nice.'

'It's lovely, Jenny,' Christine replied, unsteadily, seeing none of the uneven stitches, nor the crown made of a milk bottle top, seeing only a small girl so many years ago, her eyes wide with wonder as she looked at the fairy on the tree.

And then she saw it, under the lowest branches.

A manger, tiny and perfect. The crib, with the Baby. Mary and Joseph standing near, protective. The shepherds, with their sheep. A donkey.

'It's beautiful, Ted,' Christine said, sincerely, turning to the boy.

He flushed, but she could see that he was pleased.

'I haven't done the Wise Men,' he told her, awkwardly. 'Didn't have time.' He hesitated, and then, casually, as if it didn't matter, he said — 'I'll do them today, nothing else to do anyway.'

It sounded ungracious, almost rude, but Christine, meeting Neil's eyes, knew that this was a real breakthrough.

'Thank you, Ted,' she said to him, quietly.

'Mercy on us,' Maggie said, coming down the stairs, an old blue flannel dressing-gown wrapped around her. 'The one day you can all have a long lie, and look at you, up at this time. All right, who's helping to get breakfast ready?'

She led the way to the kitchen, and supervised the making of breakfast. To her surprise, Christine found some parcels at her place when she sat down at the table. There was one so big she had to lift it off the table, to open it.

It was the work-basket Ted had been making, and her breath caught in her throat as she saw the card, signed by all the boys.

'It's so that you can help Maggie to mend our socks,' Keith told her, cheekily. 'They've really piled up while you were away. Not that you were ever very keen on mending socks, of course.'

Christine laughed, touched beyond words as much at the warmth and affection on the faces of the boys as at the present itself.

There was a pair of bedsocks from Maggie, and there was a silk scarf from Jenny.

'It was all I could get down at the Post Office,' Jenny told her, 'but you — you always used to like blue.'

'Oh, Jenny, I love it,' Christine told her daughter, unable to say any more.

And at the bottom, there was a small

square parcel. Christine opened it, wonderingly.

It was a ring, an old-fashioned ring, tiny sapphires set into a band of gold.

'Your mother's ring, Neil,' Christine murmured, looking at it. And then, startled, her eyes met his.

'That's right,' he said softly, steadily. 'My mother's ring. You remembered that, Chris, without even trying to. I — always said I would give it to you. Let's put it on your right hand — for the moment.'

He took her right hand and put the ring on for her, and for a moment, there was nothing and no one in the room but the two of them. Christine smiled, a little uncertainly.

'You're supposed to kiss her, Doctor Neil,' one of the boys suggested.

'Good idea,' Neil agreed gravely.

He leaned across the table and kissed Christine, quickly, lightly, but the warmth of his lips lingered on hers.

'I haven't anything for anyone,' Christine said after a moment, looking round the table. 'I was thinking of Christmas, and then — with Jenny coming, and — '

And that letter from John Scott, the letter telling her, starkly, that for so many years Adam had known where she was. But she couldn't say that to anyone but Neil.

'Fine enough Christmas present for us all having you back, lass,' Maggie said, brusquely, and then she stood up quickly, glared round at everyone as if to dare them to say she was being soft or sentimental, and told the boys they'd better get breakfast washed up if they wanted her to get the turkey cooked for their Christmas dinner.

As the day went by, Christine realized that Jenny was watching her, trying to say something, but never quite reaching the point of speaking. Until it was late, and everyone but Neil and Christine and Jenny had gone to bed.

'Mum, I'm sorry,' Jenny said quickly, awkwardly. 'I — don't know what to say, really, but — the things I said before, the things I thought about you and Dr Ferguson — Mum, there's a lot I still can't understand, maybe I never will, but — if marriage means the way things are between you two, then — then maybe it isn't such a bad thing.'

She flushed, then, embarrassed.

'Thanks, Jenny girl,' Christine said softly, and the unconsciously-used pet-name from long ago made Jenny look at her, her eyes wide.

'I don't know why it all happened,' Jenny went on then, shakily, 'but — but I'm glad we're together again.'

'So am I, Jenny,' Christine replied, and now she didn't try to hide her feelings, all her heart was in her eyes as she looked at her daughter.

'I won't ever forget this Christmas,' Jenny said then, quietly.

'I won't forget it either, Jenny,' Neil agreed.

Christine watched them looking at each other for a moment, seriously, gravely, the man she loved and the daughter she loved. Then they both smiled. And Christine, in that moment, had a complete certainty that although there could still be stormy times ahead, eventually things would work out for the three of them.

If they could persuade Adam to agree to a divorce.

Talking it over, on the way to Edinburgh three days later, Neil pointed out that since this was what Adam wanted — since this was what he had wanted even ten years ago — there should be no problem.

'I know there shouldn't,' Christine agreed. She hesitated, unwilling to dampen his high spirits now that they were actually taking steps. But she had to admit to herself that she was uneasy and apprehensive. She said as much to Neil.

For a moment, his hand left the wheel and covered hers.

'I don't blame you for not looking forward to going back,' he said, comfortingly, 'but I promise you it will be all right. I won't leave you there for a second without me. Look Chris, look at it reasonably. Adam wants to marry Valerie, you want to marry me — you've been apart for ten years, and even when you were back in the house both Valerie and the housekeeper know you had your own room. There's nothing to stand in the way of it, love.'

'Mrs Howard would say anything Valerie wanted her to,' Christine agreed, slowly. 'She must have agreed to pretend I wasn't in the kitchen that day. But — I don't know, Neil, I just have this uneasy feeling. If John Scott is right, and if Adam is really afraid of the reaction to a divorce — then he isn't going to feel any differently now. A divorce is still going to cause talk.'

'But he can't go on looking at it that way for the rest of his life,' Neil pointed out reasonably. 'He can't expect a woman like this Valerie seems to be to go on waiting — I think it's amazing that she's waited so long.'

He hesitated, and then, his eyes on the road in front of them, he said, quietly, that what he really wanted to know was why Christine had thought that Jenny was dead.

'What I want to know, even more than that,' Christine replied, her voice low, 'is how he could do what he did, and leave me for all these years away from Jenny. I — I can't ever forgive him for that, Neil.'

'No, I don't think I can either,' Neil replied. 'Chris, let's stop and have that flask of coffee, and then push on.'

He pulled in to the side of the road, and brought the picnic basket forward. It was cold, so Christine poured coffee for them and they sat inside the car to drink it. Neil told her then that he had phoned John Scott and asked if they could spend a night with him.

'He meant it when he said he'd help us,' he said. 'I don't know that we'll need any help, but — he's done a lot already.' He packed their cups in the basket, and taking out his handkerchief, wiped the corner of her mouth, gently. 'You've got coffee there,' he told her.

For a moment, then, he looked down at her, unsmiling. She thought he was going to kiss her, but he didn't. Instead, he touched her cheek lightly, with one finger.

It was late when they reached Edinburgh, and John Scott's house was on the far side. Christine dozed, lightly and uneasily, for the last hour in the car, realizing that there had been a great deal to do in the last few days.

She opened her eyes as the car stopped.

'We're here, Chris — wake up,' Neil said.

Then the car door opened, and John Scott was there, a scarf around his neck.

'Come in — come in, you must be cold and hungry. Food and a fire ready for you,' he told them.

He led the way into a small and cosy room, with a hot tray beside the fire, and a casserole on it.

'My housekeeper left this before she went,' he told them. 'Help yourselves,

266

and sit down and tell me all your news. But first of all — how is Jenny?'

Christine held out her hands to the welcome blaze.

'Jenny is fine,' she told him, sincerely. 'You don't know how grateful I am that you brought her to us.' Just for a moment, the white eyebrows rose, and she realized that she had said 'us' and not 'me'. Warm colour flooded her face, but she saw that John Scott's eyes were friendly and approving.

It was only when they were all drinking tea that they spoke of the letter and the photograph.

'I could kick myself for not thinking of it right away,' John Scott apologized. 'I knew there was some thought nagging at me, but it was only after I got back here that I pinned it down. When are you going to see Adam? I take it that's why you're here?'

'That's why we're here all right,' Neil confirmed. He looked directly at the older man. 'Mr Scott — '

'Make it John, Mr Scott makes me

feel too old,' the other man said.

'John — there's a lot that we can't understand, but all that really matters is to get the present position sorted out. I don't see any difficulty — he wants his freedom and now so does Chris. It should be simple.'

'I certainly hope so,' John Scott agreed, and Christine realized that for some reason he shared her apprehensions. And yet Neil was right — there shouldn't be any difficulties.

But in spite of her anxiety, she slept well, not even disturbed by the distant sound of traffic, although it was something she was unaccustomed to. They had already decided to go early to see Adam, before he left for work.

'Will she be there — Valerie?' Neil asked as they drove across Edinburgh.

'I don't know,' Christine told him. 'I don't think so — now that Jenny has gone, I doubt if she would stay there.'

But as they turned the corner of Jenner Street, she put her hand on his arm, stopping him.

'Wait,' she told him urgently. 'That's Valerie's car now.'

She wasn't sure whether that would make it easier or harder, that Valerie would be there with Adam. All she did know was that she would have given anything in the world not to have gone into that house, not to have faced Adam and Valerie.

'Chin up, love,' Neil said quietly, and she managed to smile, grateful for his understanding.

He parked the car outside the gate and they went in, his hand firmly on her arm.

The sound of the chime bell rang through the house, and Christine could feel her heart thudding as they waited. Then the door opened, and Adam stood there.

'Christine!'

All the colour left his face, and there was something in his eyes — something that seemed to Christine almost fear, just for a moment. Then, with an effort that was obvious to her, he recovered.

'Well, this is a surprise,' he said, pleasantly. 'Do come in — my house-keeper has just gone out for some shopping, but Valerie is here. Valerie — Christine is back,' he called, and from the swift glance Neil gave her, Christine knew that he, too, recognized this as giving Valerie some warning.

And when Valerie came through, although she too was white, she was composed.

'This is quite an occasion,' she said. She looked at Neil, then. 'Aren't you going to introduce us to — your friend?'

'This is Dr Neil Ferguson,' Christine replied, amazed to find how steady her voice sounded, in spite of the uneven thudding of her heart, in spite of the cold clamminess of her hands.

Adam led the way through to the big lounge, and switched on the electric heater.

'Even with the central heating, it gets cold,' he remarked. Then he turned to Christine. 'I suppose you want to see

270

Jenny?' he asked.

Christine shook her head.

'No, Adam,' she replied, quietly. 'John Scott brought Jenny to me — you know where she is, you know where I went to.'

'Does this mean that your — memory has returned?' Adam asked.

'No,' Christine replied, and at the same time Neil said, urgently — 'Wait, Chris — don't say anything.'

But she had said it, and there was no mistake about the look of relief in Adam's eyes and in Valerie's.

'I gather you — found your way back to where you had been?' Adam asked, easily, and Christine could see that for some reason he was considerably less worried than he had been in that first moment of seeing her.

'Yes, I did, with John Scott's help,' Christine told him. And then, because it couldn't be kept back any longer, she burst out — 'Adam, how could you do it?'

'How could I do what?' Adam asked,

his voice guarded.

'Christine dear, do tell us what you're accusing poor Adam of.'

Valerie's voice was amused, reasonable, and suddenly, remembering the things Valerie had said before she left this house, Christine knew that she must keep calm and controlled.

She ignored Valerie, and spoke to Adam.

'You knew where I was, years ago, and you did nothing. All these years, I could have been with Jenny.'

'I don't know what you're talking about, Christine,' Adam replied, his eyebrows raised. 'You're the one who walked out — not me.'

And all at once it was too much for Christine. She knew that if she said another word she would burst into tears, and fling wild accusations at both of them. Then, before she could even try to speak, Neil's hand covered hers, warm and strong and reassuring.

'I'll tell you what she's talking about, Lawrence,' Neil said, and the cold anger in his voice obviously shook Adam. 'Ten years ago, when Chris left you, she left because you wanted a divorce, to marry her.' He looked at Valerie briefly, contemptuously, and Valerie turned away. 'And because she thought Jenny was dead. I want an explanation of that.'

'I don't understand what — ' Adam began, but Valerie cut in, smoothly.

'I'll give you your explanation, Dr Ferguson. Ten years ago Christine was as unstable and as neurotic as she is now — she could imagine anything.' She turned to Adam. 'I really think, Adam, it's only fair to let Dr Ruthven know about this. You know how he feels.'

'That's enough of that,' Neil said — quietly, but Valerie stopped.

'All right,' he went on, 'let's leave that aspect for the moment. But only for the moment. I'm not satisfied, and I want an explanation. And don't tell me there's anything wrong with Chris. There's something wrong, I'll grant you that. But not with Chris.'

He turned to Adam.

'Ten years ago,' he said evenly, 'you wanted a divorce. Chris wasn't prepared to give you one. She is now.'

There was a moment's silence.

'That's interesting,' Adam commented. He turned to Valerie. 'How do we feel about this, do you think?'

'Not yet,' Valerie said quickly. 'Not before the elections.'

Adam nodded.

'That's what I thought,' he agreed. 'Dr Ferguson — Valerie and I have waited a long time for what we want — we're prepared to wait a little longer. Perhaps about the end of next year?'

'So that you can get your seat in Parliament?' Neil asked, scornfully.

Adam shrugged.

'If you like to put it that way,' he replied.

Neil put one arm round Christine, drawing her closer to him.

'I'm sorry, Lawrence,' he said, clearly. 'You may be prepared to wait — we're not. Christine has had a dreadful time in the last few months, I'm not prepared to have her left like this for another year. I want divorce proceedings put under way right away, and if you won't agree to meet us, we will go ahead.'

'On what grounds?' Adam asked, smoothly, and Christine's heart sank, for he knew all to well what he was doing on the legal side.

'We'll find grounds,' Neil replied, and he looked at Valerie.

'You do that, my friend, and I'll see that Christine is found mentally unfit to see Jenny ever again,' Adam said with certainty.

Christine's heart turned over.

'Let's wait, Neil,' she murmured, sick with fear now.

'No,' Neil replied, decisively. 'This isn't going to hang over your head any longer, Chris. We're going ahead.'

He turned, then, taking Christine with him.

'Wait a minute,' Adam said, suddenly.

'I might consider this, if Christine will sign an undertaking that she will never, under any circumstances, divulge anything she knows about me to any living soul.'

Christine heard and saw Valerie's swift intake of breath, saw all the colour leave her face.

'In exchange for Jenny?' Adam suggested.

'Yes — yes, I'll sign it,' Christine said quickly.

'No you won't, Chris.'

Neil's hand on her arm stopped her.

'She won't sign anything, Lawrence. Not anything. What are you afraid of?'

'Nothing — I dislike publicity, that's all,' Adam replied. But the fear that had been in his eyes earlier was there again.

'Adam — you fool,' Valerie said, her voice low and angry.

She came across the room to them.

'You do anything to Adam, and I guarantee we'll stop Christine having Jenny. There are plenty of legal ways.'

Neil looked down at her.

'Then we'll fight you every inch of the way,' he said evenly. 'Come on, Chris.'

He said nothing until they were almost at John Scott's house, and Christine sat huddled in her seat, tears running down her cheeks.

'Stop it Chris,' he said at last, roughly, but not unkindly. 'That won't get us anywhere. Hurry up — I want to talk to John Scott about this.'

He took her into the house. John Scott was waiting for them. Quickly, concisely, Neil told him what had happened. what Adam and Valerie had said.

'There's something far wrong,' he finished, leaning forward eagerly. 'John, I don't know why, but Adam Lawrence is frightened to death of something that Chris knows. Something Chris has forgotten she knows. Frankly, I don't care a great deal what it is — all I want is for Chris to be free.'

The older man stood thinking, frowning.

'Will you let me handle this?' he asked Christine abruptly. 'I think I can get results.'

When Christine, after a quick look at Neil, nodded, he strode across to the phone and dialled a number.

'Adam?' he said briskly. 'John Scott here. Adam — first and foremost I'm a newspaperman, and I've never yet fallen down on a good story. And there's a good story here. Why did Christine leave you ten years ago? Why did you do nothing when you found out where she was? What are you afraid of Christine saying now?'

He was silent for a moment, listening, and then he shook his head.

'Not a chance, Adam — too good a story. You know I don't agree with you all the way politically in any case, so it won't bother me if you don't get in. When? Early next week, I think. I've got a fair bit to start with, and Christine and Neil are with me right now.' He laughed. 'Look out for the Star early next week.'

He put the receiver down, and turned back to Neil and Christine.

'That should bring us some results,' he said with satisfaction.

It was only later — much later — that Christine remembered that he had said this, and wondered if he would have done the same, if he could have forseen just what these results were to be.

But by then it was too late.

8

'I don't like it,' Christine said, unhappily, after John Scott had left them. 'It seems like blackmail.'

'Don't forget that John Scott has no real intention of doing this,' Neil pointed out. 'All he wants is to frighten Adam into coming into the open.' He came over and sat beside her. 'And don't forget too that blackmail is exactly what Adam and Valerie were doing — with Jenny as the bait. No, Chris, I wouldn't have too many scruples about it.'

But Christine still wasn't happy about it.

'We could have waited, Neil,' she said, her voice low.

'No, Chris.' She looked up at him, startled by the determination in his voice, by the set of his chin. 'We've waited too long already. How old are you?'

'Thirty-nine,' Christine told him.

'And I'm two years older. Chris, I want us to be married soon, I want us to have a child — more than one if possible.' He smiled, his eyes suddenly warm and teasing. 'You're blushing, love.'

'So I should be,' Christine protested, a little faintly. 'Here you are talking about us marrying, and — and having a family, and in the first place I'm still married to Adam, and in the second place — we're too old, Neil.'

'Who's too old?' he demanded, and his lips were hard on hers, his arms holding her close to him until she was breathless.

'All right, I'll take that back,' Christine agreed, laughing a little in spite of her worries. 'Neil — when did John say he would be back? We shouldn't be too long about getting back, with the roads the way they were.'

Neil looked at his watch.

'He said he'd be back about eleven, and it's almost that now.'

They packed their small suitcases in the car, and Christine filled up the coffee flask, and just as she had put the picnic basket into the car, John Scott's car drew up.

'I've got a passenger for you,' he said. 'Can you take him back with you?'

Clive got out of the car and came round to Christine.

'Mrs Lawrence — is Jenny all right? he asked, anxiously. 'Uncle John says she is, but she was in such a state when I brought her here. How is she?'

'She's fine, Clive, I promise you,' Christine told him. She looked at Neil. 'I suppose we can take Clive with us?'

'Of course,' Neil replied. 'I gather this is Jenny's boyfriend? I think it will do her the world of good to see you.'

He turned to John Scott and held out his hand.

'Thanks for everything,' he said. 'Will you let us know if there are any developments?'

'I'll do that,' the older man agreed.

'Goodbye, Christine — I hope things work out now.'

Christine kissed him, and got into the car, with Clive in the back seat, and they drove off. Before they were out of Edinburgh, Clive was asleep, looking somehow much younger and more defenceless, in spite of his beard, than he had when Christine met him first.

'He's tired out,' she said to Neil.

Neil nodded.

'He told me he's been doing two jobs through these holidays.' He glanced at her. 'He wants to save hard and ask Jenny to marry him.'

'But Jenny's only — she isn't eighteen yet,' Christine protested.

'You're not consistent,' Neil pointed out, gravely. 'First you say you're too old, then you say Jenny's too young. What would you say is the right age?' Then, serious again, he went on, 'No, I think you're right. I think Jenny has a fair bit of growing up to do. But I like this young fellow, I'd like him to be around while Jenny does her growing up.'

'I think I would too,' Christine agreed.

They stopped outside Fort William to have coffee, and Clive woke then, blinking sleepily as he drank some coffee.

'Not long now,' Neil told him. 'Just a couple of hours.'

'Do you want me to take a turn at the wheel?' Clive asked, but Neil said he didn't mind driving. And for the rest of the way, Clive leaned forward and talked to Christine about Jenny, telling her of Jenny's school days, and her first year at Art School. Christine listened eagerly, drinking it all in, filling up the gaps in the years without Jenny.

'Is she any good? At art, I mean?' Neil asked, curiously.

Clive shrugged.

'She draws well,' he said, defensively, 'and she has a good eye for colour.'

'But she isn't going to set the world

alight?' Neil asked, and Clive eventually agreed.

'She isn't mad keen about it,' he said. 'I am. Painting means more than anything else to me — except Jenny. But for Jenny — I think it was just something to do.'

It was late afternoon before they reached the pass into the glen, and they could see that there had been more snow. The last few miles of the journey took longer than they had expected, and it was dark when they drew up outside the house. The kitchen window was lit behind the curtains, but no one seemed to have heard the car.

'They'll be having supper, and driving Maggie round the bend with all the noise,' Neil told Clive. 'Let's go right in.'

He opened the door and he and Christine went in.

Keith was the first to see them.

'They're back!' he told everyone, and the boys all stood up, but Jenny was there first, her arms tight around

285

Christine for a brief moment.

'I was afraid something might have happened,' she said breathlessly, 'with the roads so bad.'

She was smiling, but Christine could see the anxiety in her eyes, and she realized, achingly, that it would be a long, long time before Jenny could learn to trust completely again.

'We brought a visitor for you, Jenny,' Neil told her, and he drew Clive forward.

Watching Jenny, Christine saw all the colour leave her face. She put out one hand instinctively, and then drew it back.

'Hello, Clive,' she said after a moment. 'I didn't expect to see you.'

Clive shrugged.

'You know how it is,' he replied, off-handed, 'you get fed up doing nothing.'

Surprised, Christine looked at Neil, but obviously if this was the way Clive wanted it, they had to leave it to him. Jenny took him off to introduce him to the boys, but Neil called Keith over.

'I rang the hospital while we were in Edinburgh,' he told the boy. 'They've got these last X-rays, and they're prepared to operate now. Wait a minute, don't get too excited,' he said hastily, 'they can't promise anything. But if it's successful, you'll be able to walk with calipers. They'll be letting us know the details soon.'

The boy's face was ablaze with happiness, and all at once there was another moment of recognition for Christine. Keith, younger, thinner, sullen and awkward when he came to them first after being put on probation for stealing. Resentful and defensive because of being crippled, with a grudge against the world. And now he was so different.

It was only the next day that Jenny asked her what had happened in Edinburgh with her father. Christine was glad that she was so absorbed in Clive — although Jenny was determined not to show that she cared one way or the other — glad to have extra time to think about what Adam and Valerie had said.

'Did he agree to a divorce?' Jenny asked.

Christine shook her head.

'Not really,' she admitted. 'Or at least not immediately.'

She didn't intend saying anything to Jenny about Adam's statement that he would consider it after the elections.

'I suppose he wants to wait until the elections are over,' Jenny said, surprising Christine. 'I don't know why he thinks a divorce will make that much difference in this day and age.'

Once again Christine's heart ached for this daughter of hers, sounding so worldlywise and sophisticated, and yet underneath so vulnerable.

'All we can do is wait and see what happens,' she said to Jenny, not mentioning John Scott's threat over the telephone to Adam.

It was Hogmanay the next day, but for Christine, with the shadow and the concern over what was going to happen hanging over her, it was strange and a little frightening to go into a New Year that held so much of the unknown in it. But Neil was more confident.

'This is going to be our year, love,' he said kissing her as the bells rang the old year out and the new year in.

He raised his glass to her, and after a moment Christine raised hers, and tried to smile.

'To us,' he said.

'To us,' she echoed. Then she saw that his eyes were concerned as he looked down at her.

'To us,' she said again, loudly, and now her chin rose, and a flame of colour blazed in her cheeks.

'That's my girl,' Neil told her, and he kissed her again.

Jenny and Clive were at the far side of the room, talking, and once Christine saw Jenny shake her head, colouring, as Clive said something.

'Forget about them,' Neil advised, 'they've got their problems and we've got ours. And they'll all work out.'

But in spite of his assurance, the next few days were anxious for both of them.

There was no word from John Scott, but just when Neil had decided they must phone him and find out, a letter came for Christine from Adam.

'I don't want to open it,' Christine said, her voice low, as she held the letter. 'You open it, Neil.'

He opened it, and they read it together. And when they had finished, Neil put the letter down on the table.

'He can't take it,' he said, and she could hear how shaken he was. 'He's so afraid of something that they are going away. What does he say?'

He picked up the letter again and read aloud from it.

'By the time you get this, Valerie and I will be in France, on our way to South America. I have arranged for a trust fund for Jenny's education, and Bailey will get in touch with you about this.

After what John Scott said he would do, there is no point in trying for a seat at the elections. My career is finished. I don't know for certain where we will go and what we will live on, but there is no use staying. Bailey will also take care of the divorce.'

That was all. If he had blamed them, if he had said this was their doing, somehow Christine would have felt better. As it was, with the facts plain and stark in the letter, she felt sick at the thought of what they had done, she and Neil and John Scott.

'Don't blame yourself, love,' Neil said quietly, watching her. 'And don't blame me, either. We shouldn't feel too sorry for him, he's only got what he deserved. If there is something in his past that bothers him so much, he is only getting his just reward for it.'

'I know,' Christine agreed. 'But — but Neil, we were happy together, once, and he is Jenny's father, after all.'

'He is,' Neil returned. 'And does he show any interest in how Jenny is, or does he try to come and say goodbye to her? No, Chris, don't waste your sympathy on him. I'm glad we've seen the last of Adam Lawrence.'

But they hadn't seen the last of Adam Lawrence.

The next day, a taxi from Fort William came. Adam came out — Adam so changed that all the breath left Christine's body when she saw him. His face was grey, and all the confidence and assurance were drained from him. Seeing him, she was glad that Jenny and Clive were out, glad even that Neil wasn't here, that she could see this broken man alone.

'Where is Valerie?' she asked him, taking him through to Neil's study.

He didn't answer until they were inside, and the door closed.

'Valerie is dead,' he told her then.

There was nothing Christine could say. She waited for him to go on.

'We were going across to France,' he said, and the lack of expression in his voice frightened her. 'It was stormy, but I've been on worse crossings. There — they said there was an accident.

Valerie fell overboard.'

'Adam — no,' Christine said unsteadily, shocked beyond words.

He looked across at her, and he was haggard.

'They said it was an accident, Christine,' he said again. 'But I don't know. She said it was my fault that things had happened this way, she said I dealt wrongly with you. She — ' He paused, and his eyes were distant, almost haunted, Christine thought. 'She said I had no right to expect her to live in some God-forsaken place with hardly any money. She said she had been prepared to wait for what we both wanted, but — without that, things were different.'

There was nothing Christine could say, but she leaned forward and touched his hand. It was cold.

Adam shook his head, as if trying to clear it.

'I loved her,' he said, almost to himself. 'I would have given up anything for her.' And then, as if remembering that this was his wife he was speaking to, he looked at her. 'I'm sorry, Christine, but that's how it was. I've always loved Valerie. I — should never have married you. I thought it was over, and then she came back.' He looked down at his hands. 'I told her that whatever else we had lost, we still had each other. But — she didn't think it was enough.'

He turned away.

'They said it was an accident,' he said again. 'They said she must have slipped. But — I don't know, Christine, I'll never know.'

In spite of everything this man had done, in spite of the years he had kept her from Jenny, Christine's heart ached for him in his sorrow and bewilderment.

'Adam — John Scott wouldn't have published anything,' she told him, sadly, wishing with all her heart that she had stopped Scott from threatening Adam. 'You don't need to go away, you can go back.'

'No,' he said, 'I couldn't. You — don't understand, Christine. I can't go back now. But it doesn't matter, not with Valerie gone.'

'Why did you come here, Adam?' Christine asked, gently.

He looked at her for a moment as if he didn't know why he had come.

'I came to say goodbye to Jenny,' he said, after a moment. 'And — there is something I have to tell you, Christine something about Jenny.'

Christine waited, and now her hands were cold as well.

'She had polio,' Adam told her. 'You nursed her until you were ill yourself, and when she was taken to hospital you collapsed,' He paused, and she could see that he was trying to marshal his thoughts. 'I had asked you for a divorce, many times, and you wouldn't, because of Jenny. Then when she was so ill, I thought — Valerie thought — if you thought that Jenny was dead, you would give me a divorce.'

Christine could say nothing.

'I didn't mean it to happen the way it did,' he said after a while, tiredly. 'I meant that after you had agreed to a divorce, after it was under way, I would tell you that she was all right, I would let you have her. But — when we told you that Jenny was dead, when I asked if you would divorce me, you said — you said how could I think of that with Jenny just dead. And — that night you went away, and you left me a note saying you would never forgive me, and you would never give me a divorce, and — other things.'

Still Christine couldn't understand fully.

'But didn't you think I would find out that Jenny was alive?' she asked him.

'Valerie had taken her away to France,' he told her dully. 'But in any case, all we wanted was a little time — just long enough for you to agree to a divorce, and then it wouldn't have mattered if you found out. I — we had planned that I would send you away to

Valerie's cottage in Galloway, as soon as you agreed.' He shook his head. 'But it doesn't matter now. You went away, and you wouldn't agree to a divorce.'

'You might have thought of giving me back my child then,' Christine said, shakily.

'I didn't know where you were for two years,' he told her, and she believed him. 'Then I saw that photograph, and I knew you were here.'

'Why didn't you do something then?' Christine asked him. 'Why didn't you ask me again about a divorce, why didn't you tell me Jenny was alive?'

He looked at her, but she thought that he wasn't really seeing her.

'I've had you watched, over the years,' he told her, obviously not realizing how this horrified her. 'By then I had my career to think about, I couldn't risk the publicity of a divorce. And you see —'

He paused, as if he had lost the thread of what he was saying, and Christine's horror and repugnance were gone in pity for this broken man.

'If I could have divorced you, it would have been all right. But there was never anything I could use against you. And then he — Ferguson — went away for two years. And when he came back, with the election in sight — '

He stood up.

'I have to go,' he said. 'Can I see Jenny? His eyes met hers. 'I have to tell Jenny why you left her.'

'No, Adam,' Christine's voice was low, pitying. 'No, you don't have to do that. Things will come right between Jenny and I without that. No, you don't have to tell her.'

Adam straightened.

'I do,' he replied, with certainty. 'I've got to live with myself for the rest of my life, Christine, without Valerie, and — with the knowledge of what I have done. This, at least, I can see clear.'

She left him then and went to find Jenny. And in spite of her pity for Adam in his dreadful sorrow, she realized that he wasn't telling her and Jenny about this so as to put things right, it was to clear his own conscience, to make it less hard for him to live with himself.

Jenny and Clive had just come in, and they and Maggie were speculating about the car at the door. Quietly, Christine told Jenny that her father was there, and that he would be going away, and wanted to say goodbye to her. And then, after a moment's hesitation, she told her that Valerie was dead, that there had been an accident. White-faced, Jenny went into the small study, and Christine told Clive a little of what had happened.

It was half an hour before Jenny came out, and Christine's heart ached for her daughter. But Jenny's head was high, and she went right to Clive, who took her in his arms and held her close, not saying anything, only holding her.

At last Jenny looked up.

'He's going now,' she said to Christine. 'Will you say goodbye to him? I — I'd rather not.'

Christine went out. Adam was just

getting into the taxi.

'Adam — have some tea or something to eat before you go,' she said, torn with pity for him.

He shook his head.

'I don't want anything. I'd rather go.' He held out his hand, and after a moment's hesitation Christine took it. 'Goodbye, Christine,' he said. 'You'll find the divorce is no problem — I left instructions with Bailey, and I phoned him today from Fort William. There — is no need now to protect Valerie, so it will go through easily and quickly. I hope things go well with you. And with Jenny. I — it's a bit late to say this, but — I'm sorry, Christine.'

'I'm sorry too, Adam,' Christine murmured, unaware of the tears running down her cheeks, wishing with everything in her that she had stopped John Scott, wishing that Valerie was still alive, that Adam wouldn't have to go through the rest of his life alone, wondering whether her love for him just hadn't been strong enough to stand up to the way their lives were to change. Wondering — and never really knowing.

In spite of the cold, she stood watching until the car was out of sight, and then she went inside. Jenny came to her, and they stood for a moment together, not saying anything. Then Jenny broke away.

'He told me, Mum,' she said unsteadily. 'He told me that you went away because you thought I was dead. How could they have done it, the two of them? She deserves to be dead.'

'Don't, Jenny,' Christine said, holding the girl close to her. 'You'll only hurt yourself by being bitter. The best thing we can all do now is to look forwards instead of backwards.'

Jenny shook her head stubbornly, but when Clive came over to her she went to him. A little later they went out, both quiet and subdued, with the two dogs beside them. Christine, sitting beside the fire, told Maggie what had happened. And when Neil's car drew up,

Maggie went out, so that Christine and Neil could be alone.

Neil strode into the room, his face grim.

'Has he gone? he asked. 'They told me in the village, and I knew it must be Adam. Where is he?'

'Don't be angry, Neil,' Christine said, shakily.

And she told him everything.

At the end, he was silent for a long time.

'Poor devil,' he said unexpectedly, and Christine's heart lifted at the compassion in his voice. 'We shouldn't have pushed him.' He looked at her. 'I think I'd better phone John Scott — he'll be feeling pretty bad about the whole thing.'

Christine never knew what the two men said on the phone, but Neil confirmed that John Scott, who had just heard, was blaming himself.

'I persuaded him to come down to us for a few days soon — give himself a break,' he said. 'I think he'll feel better if we talk things out a bit.' He asked Christine then how Jenny was.

'Shaken, of course,' Christine told him. 'But I think having Clive will help her a great deal. I — I just hope she doesn't turn to him for too much yet — they're both so young.'

'I wouldn't worry,' Neil advised her. 'Jenny's got a lot of sense, and so has Clive.'

And a few days later Christine could see that he was right, that there was no need to worry. For Jenny came to her and said that she wanted to begin training as a nurse.

'What about Clive?' Christine asked, too surprised to be tactful. But Jenny didn't pretend to misunderstand her.

'Clive knows how I feel,' Jenny told her quietly. 'We both need time.' She smiled, then, and it was the impish smile of the small Jenny that Christine remembered. 'Anyway, we'll both be in Edinburgh, so we'll see each other often — in between my nursing and Clive's painting.'

And Christine knew that she would be all right, this daughter of hers, given time and the chance to trust again.

And Ted, too. She could never be certain just what had broken through the boy's sullenness and reserve, Neil was sure it was the way she had spoken to him and the way Jenny had spoken to him. But whatever it was, Ted was gradually changing. He said to Neil that he was finished with drugs, it was a mug's game.

'And he meant it, Chris,' Neil assured Christine. 'He'll be all right.'

At the end of January Keith went off for his operation, and a few days later they heard that it had been a complete success. Jim and Tony went back to their homes, promising to write and keep in touch. Soon, Neil said, he would go to Glasgow and make arrangements for a few more boys to come.

Jenny was to start her nursing soon, and Clive had gone back. There was a letter from him every second day, and

Jenny did a lot of walking on the hills by herself, with only the dogs for company, returning with her cheeks pink and her eyes bright.

Maggie, who had been complaining bitterly about all the work, complained just as bitterly that the place was half empty, that they needed more boys. Neil and Christine laughed at her, and said she was never satisfied.

There was a letter from the lawyer, Bailey, in Edinburgh, to say that the divorce was under way, and they would be hearing from him soon.

'Everything is working out, Chris,' Neil said drowsily one evening, as they sat in front of the fire in the shabby little study.

But Christine found it hard to forget the way Adam had looked when he came to say goodbye to Jenny. She couldn't help thinking of him alone somewhere, with so many regrets. She said nothing to Neil, but she knew that he understood, and that he sympathized with her.

John Scott, when he came to them, said to her, guardedly, that a few things had turned up that seemed to show that it was a good thing Adam hadn't been elected a Member of Parliament. Christine didn't ask him for any details, but she knew that he was telling the truth, and not just trying to make them all feel better.

And when John Scott had gone back to Edinburgh, she said to Neil, with difficulty, that he was probably right, that Adam probably had deserved everything he got.

'But I still feel so dreadfully sorry for him,' she said sadly. 'And yet — for what he did to Jenny and me, I find it hard to forgive him.'

At the beginning of February, there was an even colder spell, with snow and ice throughout the glen. Jenny, waiting to start nursing, spent a great deal of her time in the barn with the boys, helping them with woodwork, talking to them, and sitting in a corner writing letters to Clive.

Christine and Maggie were in the kitchen one afternoon when one of the boys came across for more paraffin for the heater.

'It shouldn't be empty,' Maggie scolded him. 'You lot have turned it up again, and I said you were to leave it low.'

'It's mighty cold over there, Maggie,' he protested. 'But I'll tell them what the boss said.'

He went off with the tin of paraffin, grinning, ignoring Maggie's fist shaken at him.

'I told them it's no' safe when it's too high,' Maggie grumbled. 'Chris, would you no' go over and see that they fill it right? They're careless, the lot of them.'

Christine pulled her duffle coat down and opened the kitchen door. And as she went out, suddenly, terrifyingly, there was a huge tongue of flame from the window of the barn, and the next moment it was alight. In spite of the snow, the timber inside was so dry that it blazed immediately.

'Phone the police station, Maggie,' Christine shouted. 'I'm going over.'

The door was open, and the boys were running out.

'Jenny!' Christine screamed. 'Jenny — where are you?'

She wasn't there. Frantic, Christine ran to the door and pushed past the boys. One of them tried to pull her back from the blazing barn, but she pulled free and ran on.

'Jenny — where are you?'

The corner where Jenny usually sat writing was ablaze, but Christine ran towards it.

'Jenny!' she called. 'I'm coming, Jenny.'

She isn't there, Christine thought, terrified. Jenny isn't there. Where is she?

There was a moment of complete clarity then, of overwhelming realization of the truth. And then, through the flames, she saw a figure coming towards her.

'Jenny's all right — she's outside, Chris.'

It was Ted.

His face was blackened by the smoke, as he took her arm and hurried her towards the blazing doorway. And then, just as they reached it, Christine saw the beam falling — right towards them. She stumbled and fell, and knew nothing more.

★   ★   ★

She was in her bedroom when she woke, but there was no confusion in her mind. Not any more. She knew that she had fallen in the doorway of the blazing barn, and she guessed that Ted must have dragged her out.

'Mum? How do you feel?'

'I don't know,' Christine admitted, surprised to find how sore her throat was. 'Ted said you were outside — is he all right?'

'His hands are burned, but not badly,' Jenny told her. 'I was first outside, I was running to phone for help. That's why you didn't see me.'

She bent down and kissed Christine's cheek quickly, awkwardly.

'Your arm is burned too,' she said. 'The same one that was broken. But Neil says it isn't too bad, it should heal quickly.' She straightened from the bed. 'Can Ted come in and see you?' she asked. 'He's been worried about you — in spite of Neil telling him you were just sleeping off the shock.'

Neil, Christine thought as Jenny went for Ted. She says Neil so easily, so naturally now.

She wanted desperately to see Neil, because of what she had known in that moment in the barn. But first there was Ted. The boy came in awkwardly, both his hands bandaged.

'I won't stay, Chris,' he said, 'I promised Doctor Neil I wouldn't, and anyway Jenny has just phoned the surgery to tell him to come and see you.'

Christine held out her unbandaged hand to him, and he took it, with difficulty, between his own.

'We're a couple of crocks, aren't we, Ted?' Christine said, a little unsteadily. 'I just want to thank you for coming for me through that awful fire.'

'You wouldn't listen,' he told her, smiling a little. 'I tried to tell you that Jenny was all right, but you went on in. So I had to come after you.'

If he wants to play it cool, let him, Christine thought with a wave of affection for the boy.

She smiled.

'I'm glad you did, it wouldn't have been very comfortable in there in another minute or two.'

'You're darned right,' Ted agreed, with feeling.

There was a scream of brakes from down below, and the kitchen door slammed.

'Here's doctor Neil,' Ted said. 'I'll see you when you come down, Chris.' At the door, he turned round. 'I'll be going soon — my Dad wants me back again now that I'm off the stuff. But I'll write — and I'll come back and see you.'

He must have met Neil on the stairs, for Christine heard a few words exchanged before Neil came in, closing the door behind him.

He looked at her for a long time, without speaking.

'Don't ever do that again,' he said at last, unsteadily. 'I got here just as that beam collapsed on you and Ted.'

'I'm all right,' Christine assured him.

'I know,' he agreed. 'But you might not have been.'

He came over to her and sat down, taking her hand in his.

Christine took a deep breath.

'Neil,' she said quietly, 'when it's spring, will you take me fishing again at the rock pool up the head of the glen — where you first taught me to fish?'

He looked at her, and all the colour drained from his face.

'When did you remember?' he asked her after a moment.

'Just before Ted found me,' she told him. 'It was the strangest thing, Neil. I was looking for Jenny, and she wasn't there, and — and all at once the gap closed, I remembered everything. I remembered coming here first, all these years ago, so full of bitterness and unhappiness that I was prickly with everyone. And — ' her voice was low, but her eyes were steady and clear on the beloved familiarity of his face. 'And I remembered falling in love with you, and fighting it, and — you going away. And the day I came to meet you in Fort William, when you came back, I remember it all.'

He was watching her.

'And — going to Edinburgh?' he asked her.

Christine nodded.

'Yes, I remember that — that was what brought it all back.' She was silent for a moment, and then she told him. 'When I got to Edinburgh, it was raining. I decided that before I went to see Adam, to ask him about a divorce, I would go to see Jenny's grave.'

She looked up at him, and her eyes were troubled.

'He even went that far, Neil — he had told me where she was buried. I went to the cemetery, and — I couldn't find Jenny's grave. It wasn't there. I suppose the shock of that was what did it.'

She was quiet, then, remembering the awful horror of standing there in the rain, and wondering where Jenny was. Looking from one tombstone to another, and not finding Jenny.

She told Neil this, with difficulty, for the horror of it was too fresh in her mind.

'I don't know what happened next,' she admitted then. 'I remember standing there beside Adam's family plot, and I was thinking — Where is she? Where is Jenny? And then, somehow, I was looking for her in the park, and — I had forgotten everything else.'

She looked at him, bewildered.

'How can that be, Neil?' she asked him. 'The two things are both equally clear in my mind now, but — I must have left the cemetery and gone to the park, and — forgotten where I had been.'

'I told you there isn't really any explanation for these things, Chris,' Neil said slowly. 'But it bears out what I said to you before. You were at the place where you thought Jenny was buried, and there was this terrific shock of not finding her. Somehow, you couldn't take it, and you blanked out everything else, and went back years ago, to when everything was all right.'

He hesitated and then, carefully, he asked her if she remembered the last few months before she left home.

Christine nodded.

'I remember everything,' she told him quietly, sadly. 'Valerie came back from America. At first, I was too blind and trusting to see, but eventually I had to. Adam asked me for a divorce, so that he could marry Valerie, but I refused. Because of Jenny. I — don't want to think about these months, Neil, when I knew my marriage was breaking up and — and then when Jenny was so ill.

There's only one thing.'

Not looking at him, she told him what he had to know about, the thing that Adam had been so afraid about.

'It was a forgery case,' she said. 'Adam got the man off, and he knew he was guilty. He — the man gave him a great deal of money, when Adam got him off. When I left him, I said that if he ever came near me again I would bring this into the open. I threatened him, Neil — I blackmailed him just as much as he blackmailed me.'

Neil's hand tightened on hers.

'No, you didn't, love,' he told her firmly. 'You were so hurt you just lashed out with whatever weapon you could find.' He hesitated, and then he told her that this was one of the things John Scott had been suspicious about, that John Scott had told him that it looked as if there had been a miscarriage of justice, that this alone justified what they had done.

'And don't ever forget, Chris,' he said at last, 'that Adam would have let you

316

go through the rest of your life without knowing about Jenny. He would never have done anything to bring you together — unless perhaps when he was good and ready to get his divorce, when it didn't matter any more to him. Don't forget that, when you're blaming yourself.'

But Christine didn't think it would be easy to forgive herself for that. In a way, she realized with sadness, everything that had happened, all the unhappiness, all the tragedy, had happened because she had been intolerant and unforgiving to Adam. And yet — could she have done anything else? All these years ago, she had felt so strongly that divorce was wrong, that marriage was for ever. Could she have gone against her own beliefs, against everything she held to be the right thing to do?

I don't think I could have acted any differently, she thought at last. And with the thought came acceptance. Acceptance of all the years that were gone, the years that could never be recalled.

'What is it that Omar Khayyam says?' she asked Neil. 'Remember — years ago, we used to read him in the winter, sitting at the fire. The bit about the moving finger.'

'The moving finger writes, and having writ
Moves on; nor all your piety nor wit
Shall lure it back to cancel half a line
Nor all your tears wash out a word of it.'

When Neil had finished, Christine sat silent for a while. It's over, she thought, I cannot change any of it. All I can do — all any of us can do — is to go on now.

'Give me my dressing-gown, Neil,' she said. 'I'm coming down to the kitchen.'

Going downstairs, she felt a little shaky, a little uncertain of herself, but

Neil's arm was strong, and she leaned on him.

She could hear the sound of the boys talking, of Maggie telling them something, of Jenny laughing. At the window in the hall, she stopped and looked out.

The snow had stopped, and there was a pale, wintry sun trying to shine through the clouds. From that window, she couldn't see the barn, but Neil had told her it was completely burned down. But we'll re-build it, she thought, with growing strength. The boys will help, these ones and the other ones who come to us.

'Do you think winter is over?' she asked Neil, looking out at the sunshine.

He looked down at her, and she knew he was answering her unspoken thoughts.

'Not quite,' he said at last. 'But the worst of it is over. Soon it will be spring.'

Soon it will be spring.

In her mind, Christine repeated his words, thankfully, joyfully.

Soon it would be spring, and she and

Neil would be married as soon as possible. Summer, and autumn, and then winter again. And all the rest of their lives, all the seasons of their lives, they would be together.

She took his hand, and together they went towards the voices and the laughter.

THE END